WESTSIDE ORACLE (MIDLIFE OLYMPIANS #1)

A PARANORMAL WOMEN'S FICTION NOVEL

T.J. DESCHAMPS

EDITED BY
EMILY PAPER

EDITED BY
RHIANNON RHYS-JONES

To my mother, Annie. Thank you for the Wonder Woman Underoos and for having the patience of saint as I climbed and jumped all over, pretending to be Diana.
Your rambunctious little girl now writes her own heroes because you encouraged my wild imagination.
But, can you picture where I'd be if you'd relented on the Lasso of Truth?
Actually, don't.
I might have had an entirely different career.

FOREWORD

In 2020 while we were all sitting at home, waiting the virus out, I signed-up to go on a trip to Greece with a bunch of my friends. There, I stomped around the Acropolis, spent hours upon hours in the Acropolis Museum, climbed the myriad of steps to visit the mountain top monasteries of Meteora, stopped by where 300 Spartans fought Xerxes forces, shopped and ate in the village of Arachova, spent a day at the ruins of Apollo's temple in Delphi and touched the stone where the real-life women who served as Oracles sat upon a tripod.

I listened to lectures from my tour guides, asked museum docents countless questions, took notes, and then while I sat poolside in sunny Mykonos, started jotting down ideas for a new trilogy. In Santorini, I decided the story would be of a Greek immigrant.

When I came home, I delved into books on Greek mythology: scholarly tomes, fun mythology monster guides, godly family trees. I also hit up some history books to double-check what I'd learned there. Always double-check!

I hope my hard work paid off and this book is as epic and timeless as any Homeric endeavor.

CHAPTER

ONE

Sometimes one bad decision can throw you off-course for life, leading you to one misery after another. Sometimes the Fates help you out with a metaphorical cuff to the ear.

When the Fates decided to give me a smack, I was eating a sandwich and deliberating whether I should leave my husband, Carlo. The sandwich was the same kind I'd been eating for a week straight: mayonnaise, tomato, and white bread. The man was the same con artist I'd married at seventeen.

Next to my lunch, a stack of bills piled an inch thick lie on the folding card table that served as my desk in the tiny storeroom of my divination shop. Carlo had told me he'd take care of the bills last month. He had not. In fact, he hadn't paid a single bill in three months.

I ate my sandwich and prepared for the inevitable fight. The stack of bills, girding my loins so to speak.

The physical evidence of his lies would help quash any gaslighting, but not by much. It could be snowing out and Carlo would try to convince me it was a balmy summer day, if it benefited him to do so.

Part of me was sick of living like this, but the edge was all I'd known since I started running with Carlo in my teens. I didn't think I'd be able to handle the typical middle-aged mom life, nor would I like it. Not that I had a choice.

Pregnant at sixteen and married by seventeen, I was technically a middle-age mom, but nothing about my life had been typical.

I just wished reading fortunes was as lucrative as it had been when I was young. I blame the small, seaside town. The locals either trusted me by now or not. Thanks to Carlo, mostly not. Tourist season would bring more clients and cash, but that wouldn't be for a few more weeks.

Carlo needed to fork over cash. Tonight.

The bell on the storefront rang, alerting me that someone who needed to know their future *now* had entered the shop.

I smiled. Maybe I wouldn't have to fight Carlo after all.

Things might be about to turn around.

The sign on the front read: Madame Francine, Seer. In slightly smaller, less stylized print it read: Walk-ins Welcome! In even smaller print it read: Scheduled Readings Half Price.

Giving my regulars a discount, or rather what they perceived as a discount, garnered loyalty, and I didn't mind them paying less if they were paying regularly in the off season. As their fortune teller, I was counselor, priest, best friend, mother, and sister to many of my clients.

However, this was someone new. I could feel it in my bones the way I knew Carlo would score big or small. The way I knew a sale on necessities would happen before it was announced.

Maybe tourist season started a little early. Here's to hoping a rich out-of-towner was willing to pay for extras.

I placed my tomato and mayonnaise sandwich on a paper plate, dusted the crumbs off my hands, rose from my metal folding chair at the rickety card table, and went through the beaded curtains from the back of the shop to the front.

The woman in the front took me in as I took her in, each of us assessing for our own reasons. I saw what I needed to.

Her hair had been blonde in her youth but had turned a pretty silver in recent years. More importantly, she had paid top dollar to have a late Jackie O' cut. She must have had work done on her face or Botox kept her skin smooth because she didn't have a single crow's foot, laugh line, worry line creasing her forehead, or any sunspots— not even on her hands.

That struck me as odd. Women of that age sun-worshipped way too much and sat in cigarette smoke filled spaces most of their lives, and their hands usually gave away their real age when their faces didn't.

I shrugged internally. What did I care? She was obviously loaded.

Real diamonds sat in her ears, dangled from a thin chain, and adorned her fingers—the diamonds were plentiful but not overly large. Lots of birthday, Mother's Day, and Christmas gifts, most likely, but some of them looked to be inherited older pieces. Her neutral-colored clothes were subdued, but classic in their elegance and style. Definitely designer made, judging by the material.

Not only did she possess fancy jewels and nice duds, she had a body that screamed she had a personal trainer. Women thicken in their late years. I know I did. She looked like she could compete in a triathlon.

The shoes were the clincher. To the untrained eye, they were taupe kitten heels. Nothing to brag about. To someone who was trained by the best conman around and who studied the top fashion lines from midcentury nineteen hundreds until the most recent season of the 2020s, I knew those shoes were so rare they should be in a museum.

I sighed, envious of that kind of money covering her feet. I could pay off all my bills and a few months' rent on my building with those shoes. Her outfit and jewelry would allow me to sit pretty for long time.

I had to play my cards right. The potential client wasn't upper middle-class bourgeois, she possessed multigenerational *wealth*. My heart raced with the thrill of what I could squeeze from her.

The corners of her mouth turned downward as she finished her inner deductions about me, and my heart sank a little.

Yeah. I disappoint me, too.

I was wearing a thrift store muumuu and a feather boa. My jewelry was knock-off faux ancient Egyptian, and my makeup was overly done. It was a Madame Francine costume rather than an actual outfit.

The real bits of me weren't anything to brag about either. I had possessed gray-streaked, dark brown hair that doesn't know how to behave. At the moment, my wild curls were tied back so they wouldn't get in my food. Fine lines from laughter etched the corners of my eyes and around my mouth. A few deeper lines of worry between my brows stood out more. I liked to call myself curvy, my husband called me voluptuous, but jerk wads liked to call me fat. I mean, I wasn't offended by the word per se, body positivity and all, but fat was the low hanging fruit of insults for dimwits.

I plastered on a warm smile, widening my eyes a little too for innocence. "Welcome, please sit. Are you looking to find answers regarding family, friends, finances, or romance?"

The F-Trinity were my usual suspects. I guessed this lady wanted to know if a husband was cheating with a secretary or should she have gone for that younger man herself after being recently widowed. Either way, I'd tell her to only trust a man far as she could throw one. That advice usually rang true.

I KNEW it to be the case for the asinine man who called himself my husband. I pushed the thought of Carlo aside. Focusing on the client's problems always helped me forget my own. At least, for a little while.

"Hello, my name is Dione Dodona. I am looking for the daughter of a dear friend of mine. You are Lydia, I presume?" Her voice was smoky and deep, and there was a trace of accent coloring her words.

An accent I hadn't heard since my Greek grandparents passed when I was fifteen.

Dread pooled in my stomach. There was no way she could have possibly known my mother. I narrowed my eyes but kept smiling.

"The sign says Madame Francine. Francine Lawless is my name."

She pushed up real Dior circa 1960s sunglasses, revealing deep brown irises set in lovely bedroom eyes.

"Really? Too bad. I have an inheritance letter for Lydia Kourakos."

I licked my lips. This had to be a trap. I hadn't gone by that name since I was a teenager. I've had quite a few names since, but no one alive knew me by that name.

"Are you a cop? You have to tell me if I ask."

At least, that's what television had taught me.

The woman laughed, a rich and melodic sound. Everything about her was too perfect. I thought women like her only existed on screen. Probably a Fed with a rich politician husband or something like that. I hadn't done anything to warrant federal investigation, but I couldn't say the same for Carlo.

I stuck out of his business, and he stuck out of mine.

"Oh. You're serious? No, no. I am not a mortal authority, only a friend of Apollonia Kourakos."

The jig was up, if she knew my mother was Apollonia. I shook my head. "You couldn't possibly know her. My mother has been dead since I was four. There's no inheritance."

Sadness touched her dark eyes. She stepped forward, placing her hand over my trembling one. I normally didn't let people I didn't know touch me, but there was such warmth in the gesture, such kindness, I didn't feel the usual urge to pull away.

"No, Lydia, she didn't die in that fire, but she did have to flee. "

"There was a police report. They found her remains."

A grin touched Dione's mouth, there and gone. "Surely one such as yourself would know such things could be faked or the right officer bribed, especially in the late nineteen seventies."

None of this made sense. My mother was a runaway teenaged

mom, barely eking out a life when she died. She simply didn't have the resources to do any of that let alone have a wealthy woman talking about inheritance.

Besides, *I* had inherited my grandparents' estate, not my mom. It wasn't much. Carlo had squandered the sale of their restaurant and house money a long time ago.

"I know it's hard to believe, but your mother became something greater than her humble beginnings. Her duties kept her away from you but do know that she kept you close to her heart."

She said more, but I didn't hear her.

I was four years old, again...

My nose hurts and my eyes sting. It's so hot. I'm crawling on the floor of the room we share in the shelter. Mama is nearby. I can hear her voice. I crawl in the direction of her voice. I'm almost to her. I feel it.

Strong hands lift me. A grown up has me in his arms. He's big and strong. He smiles down at me, and I feel safe. We move so fast. I'm giddy and scared at once. Then he's putting me down.

Wings. Golden Wings spread behind his back. He runs fast again and then he's flying.

I reach my hand toward the sky, wailing for him to come back.

As a child, I'd believed I had a guardian angel for years. That's what my grandmother told me. Then I thought I'd imagined it. I remember his clothes weren't long flowy robes like angels. He had on runner's clothes. He smelled like aftershave and laundry detergent.

Recently, supernaturals have admitted they exist. Perhaps he was an angel or a fae living in the shelter and simply helped a crying kid get out of there, taking off before he had to explain how he made it out of the fire. Maybe he saved my mom, too. Took her away somewhere.

"Was my mother involved with supernaturals?"

Confusion flittered across her face—I hadn't shared my memory. Dione recovered, spreading her hands and her mouth in a broad smile at the same time. "That's what I'm here to explain. You come from a long line of women known as Oracles. First prophetesses for Zeus and then, for his son Apollo."

"Oracle? I'm sorry." I waved my hands, wanting nothing to do with this and then pointed to my crystal ball and divination tool shelf. "I'm not a real seer. Those are props I got at shops. I give advice but don't actually see the future."

The woman's smooth brow furrowed as her gaze wandered around the room, her confusion clear. "If you do not receive prophetic visions, how do you run this business?"

Restraining to not roll my eyes, I replied, "I read people and carefully listen—not just to what they say, but their clothing, their posture, and mannerisms. Then, I give them advice."

Usually, I'd pretend to channel the spirit of a friend, or a dead loved one, but she didn't need to know the details of my con.

She considered what I'd told her. After this revelation, I fully expected Dione to condone me and say this was all a mistake. Instead, she revealed the whitest teeth. "Giving advice to mundane mortals is part of being an Oracle, but not all. You would become a servant to the Olympians, and an enemy of their enemies."

"Wait. Are you asking me to join some ancient Greek Super Friends group or something?"

She laughed, a rich and melodic sound. "You would be a holy priestess and live as such. You would foretell the future. Through your temple and prophecies, you will help guide mortals to once again believe in the Olympians as deities and teaching them how to worship the Olympians in the old ways."

I barked a laugh. "Not happening. I'm no goody-two shoes Holy One. That's a con I can't pull."

Dione's eyes lit up like wicks of candles. The sharp look she shot in my direction actually hurt.

I doubled over, pain searing my guts. The agony stopped almost as quickly as it began.

Dione rushed to my side, trying to help me into a rickety wicker chair that smelled slightly of cat urine. I didn't own a cat but had found chair on the side of the road marked "free" a few days ago. The smell helped wake me up.

"I forget what my anger can do to an Oracle." She handed me a glass of icewater. "Here. Drink this."

I stared at the glass, unable to recognize it. "Where did this come from?"

Something passed over her face. Amusement? Condescension?

"You're not ready for that answer."

I scoffed, setting the glass on the table. I wasn't born yesterday. Taking food and drink from gods was never a good idea. The act bound you to them in some way. "I'm not ready to be some servant of the gods. I'm just an ordinary person, trying to get by in a crooked world."

"Apollonia said the same thing when your aunt in Greece passed." Dione grinned, but there was a touch of sadness behind her eyes, too. "You look and sound so much like your mother."

Forty years. She'd had over forty years to know my mom, and I only had four.

The hole left in my chest the night of the fire ached. My mother, a woman I only remembered from my late grandparents' pictures, was alive until recently and now gone. I didn't know the version of her that looked like me. I certainly hadn't looked like the old, faded Polaroids from the nineteen-eighties. Orphaned all over again at forty-four.

Tears pricked the back of my eyes. I sniffed, pulling it all back in. Folding my arms across my chest, I asked, "So, what did I inherit, exactly? Besides some position that I don't even know that I want."

"Being an Oracle to the gods is a harder role to accept at your age. You have a bit of wisdom to know that it won't be easy and that you should be fairly compensated. As far as inheritance, your mother owned a beautiful old Victorian in Milagro Bay, a small town in Washington state. The house is near the Olympics, where there is a formerly hidden temple, but far enough so she had her privacy." She held out an envelope. "This is the deed. You own it free and clear. She left you a financial nest egg as well. The details about that are in there. The Olympians pay in gold should you decide to become the Oracle."

I lived in a small coastal town in the south. Washington state was on the other side of the country. The only things I knew about Washington was that Seattle had a grunge music scene in the 90s and that the area currently had supernaturals exposing their powers in viral videos.

Some of those monsters were as smoking hot as they were terrifying. I'd be living close to a hotbed of magical beings and interacting with gods. I didn't know if I wanted anything to do with that, family calling or not.

"Unfortunately, my time here is up. This is all the information you'll need until the Herald presents you with the choice of becoming Oracle." Dione placed a card and a large envelope on the table next to my crystal ball. She smiled ruefully. "No matter if you pick up your mother's mantle or not, I wish you the best, Lydia, daughter of Apollonia."

CHAPTER

TWO

Soon after Dione left, my husband walked in. Carlo was a distinguished sort of handsome, in the way that men unfairly get better looking with age. The skin that had terrible acne when we were kids had cleared up. A neatly trimmed beard covered a few scars he'd possessed from that period. His dark, curling hair was peppered with silver and his Mediterranean olive skin looked good with his button-down shirt and slacks.

The man never had a wrinkle or a stain. He was always neat, compulsively so. He never put it on me though. Carlo had all his clothes dry-cleaned. It cost him an arm and a leg, but he never asked me for a cent to cover it.

We were both kids from the rough side of a New Jersey town. Him, the grandson of Italian immigrants. Me, the granddaughter of Greek immigrants.

I got pregnant in high school. Sixteen, just like mom. Unlike whoever my biological father had been, Carlo had stuck around. Mostly. He ran with some rough guys and never grew out of that phase. He'd never had a job, but he'd always contributed to our expenses. He was proud of being an earner but never liked me asking how he got any of his money.

So, I never asked what Carlo did for a living. For the sake of our marriage, and my own sanity and my irrefutable innocence, there were a lot of things about my husband I didn't ask about.

I stuffed the papers from Dione back into the envelope she gave me. Stealthily, I slid her card off my table into a bag at my feet.

He wouldn't squander this inheritance. As soon as I could figure out the details, I planned to sign it over to our son. Luke would make it a nice retirement and get-away-from-Carlo plan for me.

His eyes followed my movement. "What do you got there?"

"Bills." I gestured toward the back. "Got a whole stack of them back there, too."

He stiffened slightly but kept walking inside. "I'm working on that."

"Thought you were going to be out earning until late, babe." *Get out of here so I can read this in peace.*

"Yeah. I am. Forgot something." His dark-eyed gaze shot to the large manilla envelope Dione had left with me. "What's that you got there? That don't look like a bill. Not the right kind of envelope."

I flicked my wrist dismissively. "Some bored housewife trying to get me to join her essential oil sales team. I took the materials to humor her."

Something was off about him. Usually, he would get all defensive if I suggested he wasn't pulling his share of the weight. At the very least, he'd start insulting me to deflect.

"Suckers love their cure-alls." Carlo shook his head in, smirking as he walked past me into the back. From the storage room, he added, "Trash those papers. Nobody makes money in those MLMs, but the top. That's why they call them pyramid schemes. Easy money though if you come up with one yourself."

My heart raced. I've never lied to my husband before, but I couldn't let him know about any of this. If I decided to accept, he wasn't coming with. "Uh huh."

My phone rang. I recognized the number and grinned. "Hey, Lukie's calling. Want to say Hi?"

It was a long shot. The two hadn't spoken in years. They'd had a falling out over some things when Luke was a teenager, and neither were about repairing it.

Carlo smiled, but it didn't reach his eyes. "Nah. I got to get going. The guys are waiting."

I waved and picked up the call.

"Heya, Lukie."

"Your husband around?"

The door shut behind Carlo.

"No. You just missed him. Did you actually *want* to talk to him?"

After a loud exhale that sounded like he was letting out some frustration, my son replied, "Nah. I never want to talk to him, ma. Not until he apologizes. I want to talk to you."

I was not surprised. Their rift didn't bother me anymore. I gave up hope of their reconciliation a long time ago and focused on damage control for my part in it all.

"What's up, sweet pea?"

Luke might be grown, but he was my star boy. Carlo and I made sure he got the best education and wanted for nothing. Usually, kids like that turned out spoiled, thinking the world owed them but not our Luke. He worked hard and got good grades, a full ride to a tech college out west. At twenty-eight, he had a career in the San Francisco Bay area making more money than Carlo or I ever dreamed of having.

I was so proud of my sweet, happy boy. It hurt to hear him upset. I hoped his partner Juan didn't break up with him. Juan was a model and prone to dramatics, but a nice kid.

"I got a new job with a tech company in Seattle. It pays really well. I bought a condo in West Seattle. I got room." He paused for a breath, his exhale loud in the phone's speaker. "I can—I can afford to take care of you. I think you should retire, and come out and live with me, ma."

My gaze dipped to the bag with the inheritance information. "What about your dad?"

"Ma, he has other women. He gambles your money all the time. His crew is involved with illegal stuff. You put up with him because he stayed when he didn't have to, but ma, he's the one that benefitted. You took good care of him, and he squandered all over your efforts. Don't say a word, just pack your bags while he's out with his boys and leave him. I'll wire you the money to buy a plane ticket."

My eyes stung. I thought we'd sheltered Luke from Carlo's doings. Carlo was always careful to say, 'the club' instead of 'the track'. I knew about the women and the other stuff. Carlo never threw it in my face. Guys in his friend set all had wives and a side chick, and the wives and the mistresses made sure to steer clear of each other. Once in a while, a side chick would think she'd become bosswife by sabotaging the actual wife. Getting in her face, saying awful stuff in front of the kids. Suddenly the troublemaker would disappear, and the real wife would get a shiny new something to make up for it. We'd never hear from the other woman again.

I'd wanted to leave for a long time, but you don't leave someone who stayed when they didn't have to, right? You don't leave when he's involved with the kind of people that could track you down and make you disappear like those troublesome women, either.

Except I had people even more powerful on my side now. You got connections, Carlo? I have literal gods. And. So. Much. Money.

"Alright."

"Alright?" Luke didn't hide his shock from his voice. "You mean it? You'll get on a flight tonight?"

I could hear a squeal in the background. That'd be Juan.

I grinned ear to ear. It would be nice to see them on a regular basis, but on my own terms. "I'm coming, but I'm not flying. I have your great-grandparents' heirlooms. I can't just let an airline lose them, sweetie."

There was a brief pause, before Luke blew out his breath. It sounded more relieved than frustrated. "Alright, ma. Text me when you have a plan."

~

I EXAMINED THE PAPERWORK AGAIN. I had a building, a bank account with more money than I'd ever dreamed of, and a fortune-telling business similar to the one I ran. It was too good to be true.

When I went back to plan my escape from Carlo, that's when I noticed another envelope on the card table. It had my name on the front.

Opening the envelope, out spilled Carlo's wedding ring, a piece of lined paper with handwriting on it, and an official looking document.

Heart thrumming in my ears, I picked up the official looking document. As I scanned the legalese, laughter mixed with relief bubbled up in my throat, bursting out in a raucous cackle.

Carlo annulled our marriage in the Dominican Republic weeks ago. Some fishing trip with the boys! I couldn't muster anger for the lie. What was important was that he did it before I received my inheritance letter. I wouldn't owe him half of anything. By being a dirty sneak, he'd done all the work for me.

More importantly, I didn't have to sneak away. He left me.

I really ought to feel sad about it. Shouldn't I?

I debated whether I wanted to read the Dear John or not. It was over. What did it matter? Part of me didn't care. Part wanted to know what I did to deserve a breakup letter after twenty-eight years.

Fran,

You always desserfed better than what I could of give you. I need to lie low for a while, and you're too good of a person for that kind of existanse. Find the kind of man who works a 9-5. A man like our grandfather's.

I never could be that, and you deserfed better than what I can awfer, which is nuttin but gray hares and worry.

Love,

C

P.S. The ring should set you up with some cash for a bit. Keep your chin up. You'll come up smelling like rose. You always did.

I snorted, crinkling up the paper. "You should have spent the ring money on some spelling and grammar lessons, Carlo."

Something deep inside me twisted. Not anger or hurt, that felt different. This was the knot that warned me something bad was going to happen.

If Carlo had to "lie low" without me, he definitely had done something serious...and got away with it. I couldn't imagine the forty-four-year-old running a bank heist. Carlo had plantar fasciitis in his feet and sciatica in his hip—not to mention high blood pressure. There'd be no waving guns around or literal running from the cops. The man wouldn't make it a block.

Whatever Carlo did, it had a big score and a big risk. Which meant I had to get out of here sooner than I'd hoped.

Everything, the rental building, the car, the bills were all in the false name we came up for me. Francine Lawless. Yeah. Even I know that was bad, but we liked Xena: Warrior Princess at the time, and Lucy Francine Lawless is bad ass.

I could have dropped the false me and been the real me. He'd left me, but he was looking out. The ring was a warning to use the money I got from a pawn and get out.

Ice cold dread filled me. I got on the banking app and checked my account. Not a dime. It was even in overdraft!

My phone rang. It was the wife of one of Carlo's crew, Renee.

"Hello, Francine? Can you believe the stunt they pulled on us?"

I shook my head. Realizing she couldn't see me, I said, "What stunt?"

Better to play stupid in these things.

"They ran the biggest scheme yet. Scamming little old ladies to sign off their life's savings to live in some swanky retirement village that was 'monster proof.' Our husbands took off to the tropics with close to a seven hundred million, Fran, dollars!"

My gaze dropped to the wedding ring, rage filling my belly. Part of me wanted to find Carlo and make him pay for leaving me with nothing. Part of me was relieved I'd never hear from him again.

We'd been going through the motions for years. Our marriage had died slowly, bleeding out from a thousand tiny cuts. Well, that wasn't entirely true. I had done my share of small, hurtful things, likely fixable with some counseling and changed behavior on my part, but Carlo had left some gaping wounds with his actions.

The thing was. I didn't know who I was without him, or without my role as wife and mother. Fran, Carlo's wife. Fran, Luke's mom.

Madame Francine, the fortune teller who couldn't see her own future going so poorly.

Conmen were charming instead of sincere. Carlo had charmed the pants off and all the savings out of me. I'd thought of myself as the charlatan. He even said I ran my own hustle. However, there was a big difference between charging people to tell them what they wanted to hear and swindling old people out of their retirement.

I was better off without him. Why did my chest ache so?

CHAPTER

THREE

Sometime after midnight, the door to the shop and all the windows of my building rattled with the force of a person knocking. On the street below my apartment window, a resonant voice shouted, "Police! Open up!"

Upstairs in our apartment, I'd thrown as many clothes and toiletries as I could into a suitcase.

In less than two minutes, they'd bring a ram, and I'd have no hope of escaping charges of aiding and abetting a wanted criminal.

I had a real problem with time management. As soon as I'd read the Dear John from my so-called husband of the past twenty-eight years, I should have fled this place with the clothes on my back. Carlo was always waiting until the very last minute to wrap-up a con.

Instead of leaving, past me had carefully packed all the things I'd inherited from my papús and yayá—evidence of my grandparents' life back in their mountain village of Arachova, Greece. I wouldn't ever let those things go. Memories of my immigrant grandparents, a weaver and a goat herder turned family restauranteurs, were my last piece of normalcy I could cling to, and no one was going to take that core of me away.

With as much as I could carry in two backpacks and two suitcases, I climbed the stairs to the roof of the two-story building. In the alley, cops shone flashlights into my windows. The first floor held my business, my livelihood. I hated to leave it behind—some of my clients relied on me for emotional support - but I had to.

I flung one suitcase and both backpacks to the roof of the building next door. Then I rubbed my sore shoulder. "I'm too old for this mess."

At my age, who would expect to be jumping rooftop to rooftop, running from the cops? Not young me, the dreamer. I thought I'd be retired by now, spending my time baking and weaving like my own grandma, not a fugitive on the run.

I hesitated a moment before throwing the suitcase with my grandparents' memorabilia. None of it was valuable, or Carlo would have pawned it by now, but the belongings were priceless to me. If they fell, I didn't know if I could continue. The belongings were all I had of my legit life before that man. They felt like an integral part of me, my family, and our heritage.

Didn't stop me from throwing them.

"One, two, three!" I heaved the suitcase over the alley.

The distance between my two-story rental and the building next store was a laughable couple of feet. Yet, I was well over forty years old, not a nimble twenty-something. I backed up and took off in a run. My arms and legs pinwheeled as I hurtled through the air like a middle-aged, lumpy cannon ball. The landing wasn't soft nor graceful and my face took its fair share of the impact.

Right about now, I seriously regretted my life choices.

"That was...egregiously awful, Lydia," a warm tenor with a hint of accent and an abundance of amusement declared.

Despite my pain and wallowing in self-condemnation, I recalled that voice. It was one that I could never forget. That voice had once said, "It's okay. You're safe with me, Lydia."

It was the voice of my hero, my savoir. The voice of my dreams for forty years. Unlike other men in my life, he hadn't lied. I had been safe, but my life had changed forever.

Disbelief warring with curiosity, I lifted my throbbing head. In the light and shadow, I made out a tall silhouette of a man. Tall and majestic as in my memory.

I had to be hallucinating. The trauma was too much to handle.

Swiping a hand over my face, I rolled over. Everything hurt, but I mustered the strength to sit up. I rubbed my eyes to get a better look.

My erstwhile childhood savior gathered my suitcases and set them upright. Same lithe, runners build. Same shorts, tank, and sneakers. Same dark hair that curled around his ears and nape. Same golden wings.

Here at my darkest hour again, the subject of my every fantasy offered me a hand for the second time in my life.

My heart fluttered. Such a silly thing in such a dire circumstance. I knew better to trust that feeling let alone have it for any man, but I couldn't help it. When you were the one who was everything to everyone, a helping hand is valued much higher than someone who has support. Besides, he wasn't a man. He had wings.

Even in the dim light of the town below and moon above, the man who'd filled my dreams for thirty years was handsome. Unconventionally so. He had a strong jaw and dark slashes for eyebrows. They scowled really well, I assumed, amused. His nose was prominent but didn't overwhelm his face. His lips possessed a sensual shape, but they weren't overtly plump like Carlo's pouty mouth. Most importantly—and disturbingly—he looked *exactly* the same as he did when I was four years old.

Something about that was both comforting and made my stomach bottom out. I understood Dione wasn't human. Her death glare had the actual possibility of murder, but she'd had such a wealthy-older-relative vibe.

I took his hand, wincing at the way my palms stung. Achieving a modicum of decorum, I decided to give this hottie whatever-he-was, who came into my life at turning points twice, a piece of my mind.

"You watched the whole thing and didn't say, 'Hey, let me fly you over here?'"

His eyes flared and then quickly recovered with a grin.

Fluttering butterflies. Again. Damn it.

"You're not a little child anymore. You could do it on your own."

The disappointment in my erstwhile savior sank deep in my gut. I'd believed that I was special and good, and that this "angel" chose me because of that. It got me through some dark times, even when I was too old to believe so. *"Suck it up, buttercup,"* stung more than my husband of twenty-eight years popping out of my life.

Maybe because I knew Carlo, like everyone else, would either die or leave me. I'd thought this man would be forever a hero. *My* hero.

"Point taken." I gripped the handles of my luggage and extended the arms, rolling them away from him. "Well, this has been fun. See you again next crisis? Maybe you can just skip it."

He followed me. Persistent bastard. "You need to believe that you don't need me and that you're powerful on your own, Lydia, or this journey will end in your demise."

"What's it to you what I believe? Matter of fact, who are you to care whether I live or die?"

He tilted his head, curious or considering, I didn't know. My erstwhile guardian angel wasn't as easy to read as the Joe and Jill Schmoes that entered my shop. Especially since it was dark.

Below, I heard someone calling for a battering ram. Have fun with that, pigs! I left Carlo's letter out so they would know I had nothing to do with his latest scam. I left my phone wiped of all data and fried by a dunk in the sink. That was nothing but a tracker anyway. I had a burner that I had loaded my data onto before switching it to airplane mode. Earlier today, I'd purchased a plane ticket to Boston with one of Carlo's cards. Francine was supposedly from Boston. I left the ticket purchase open on my computer. That would throw the fuzz off for at least a few days while I made my escape west.

I rolled my suitcase onto the ledge. Not far to the next building. Three more jumps, and I could take the fire escape into an all-night laundr-o-mat and grab the bus on the corner. I wouldn't be the only middle-aged lady who'd just got a load done after finishing her second shift, I'm sure.

"I really hate turnover. The new Oracle always brings a lot of turmoil. She needs to be trained and guided through learning the ropes. I'm the herald so I have to deal with the new ones." He threw up his hands in exasperation. "I'm finished with onboarding the new girl because the last didn't understand the risk involved with this so-called honored position. It's tiresome."

"Herald? Let me guess, you're Hermes?" I eyed his sneakers. "I thought you had wings on your sandals and a little hat, not on your back."

Hermes released an exasperated breath. He even went so far as to throw a forearm to his forehead dramatically. "Not that misconception again."

I snort-chuckled at this ancient being's antics.

"Just because humans imagine a god one way doesn't mean we look that way. Unlike the ascended, I have some autonomy. The winged sandals were symbolic because I'm fast and can travel between worlds easily. Mundanes were landbound and didn't understand at the time." He spread his hands. His sneakers became winged sandals and a gold hat with wings appeared on his hair. "Like this better?"

"Eh." I was impressed with what he could do, but not the look. Hermes was much more attractive than the depictions of him.

The illusion faded almost as fast as he created it.

I paused. "Wow. Neat trick."

After seeing the seedy side of life since I married Carlo, there wasn't much that still surprised me. I had seen transformations of supernaturals on the internet, but not something like this in real life.

"Did you make that real or just an optical illusion?" I asked over my shoulder as I inserted the handle back into the first suitcase.

"What are you talking about?"

I heaved the first suitcase onto the roof of the next building. "The winged sandals and hat thing. Were they real or did you trick my eyes with magic?"

"I am a god, " he replied with all the mystery and ethereal majesty he could throw into each word.

Second handle in, I threw the suitcase. My whole body was going to be a mess in the morning. I retrieve a bottle of ibuprofen from my purse, dry-swallowed a few, and then nodded at Hermes. "Optical illusion then."

He watched me with confusion as I backed up to get a running start. "What makes you say that?"

"Easier to trick the eyes than manifest something that doesn't exist." I pushed myself to run, thighs burning, and I hurdled again.

I miscalculated.

FOUR

The very moment I realized I'd fallen short of the mark; my life flashed before my eyes.

Early childhood had very few actual memories, but there were the ones from photos that came. Growing up with Greek grandparents of an older generation had been both wonderful and trying. If they hadn't died in my teen years, I doubted Carlo would have ever wormed his way in my life months later.

Predators didn't go for animals deep in the pack. They went for the strays straggling behind. Easy pickings are good pickings.

My stomach rocketed into my throat. My hands and feet desperately sought for purchase only to find none.

This was it. I was going to die.

I was going to die and all I could think was Hermes would have to onboard another Oracle. Woe was Hermes.

I was going to die, but that was hilarious.

My hair caught on something, halting my descent. Pain spiked in my scalp as a hand groped at my left boob and then caught my arm. The pressure released from my scalp as another iron grip caught my other arm.

Hermes cursed in Greek as he lowered me ungently to the ground. After wobbling around like a newborn giraffe for a moment, I found myself standing in the alley.

I threw my hands up in exasperation. "Great! My bags are up there."

Hermes took off again.

"Figures."

I rubbed my sore arm and the boob he'd accidentally groped. The saddest part was that awkward slip was the most intimate contact I'd had in a while. By accident was *not* the way I wanted to have my hair pulled or tit squeezed.

Oh, well. I needed to get my bags. The bottom of a fire escape was just out of reach. I stretched and got on my tippy toes. I even tried hopping like a manic ballerina. Finally, I blew out my breath. "Not happening."

My head, my boob, and my face hurt too much—not to mention my knees *and my face*. I wanted to go home and take a long soak in the tub, but I couldn't because my hu—*correction*—ex-husband was a criminal.

A giant lump sailed from the roof, becoming more distinct as Hermes and my suitcases.

"I apologize for any injury I may have caused, but seriously, you couldn't expect to make several jumps in your condition."

I scrunched up my face. Carlo made it clear he'd noticed the weight I'd put on over the years. Eventually, I made it clear he didn't have to waste his time grunting and boring me to death if he didn't like it. If I didn't take that treatment from a mediocre man, I wasn't about to take pointing out my human imperfections from a god. It just wasn't fair.

"Before I clock you for disrespect, what are you saying, exactly?"

Hermes scowled. "You need better spatial awareness, and the physical strength and agility which comes with training."

"Oh." Extending the handle for each rolling bag, I said, "I

thought oracles sat on their butts in Delphi, eating laurel leaves and inhaling fumes."

"Thousands of years ago, yes. There's been an imbalance in the belief system of this world for far too long. That's changing and the angels will at some point retaliate. You must be prepared to defend yourself."

"Oh." I shook my head. "I've got nothing to do with all of that."

"Of course, you do. You're an Oracle."

Hermes followed me down the alley while I peered around the corner of the building to see what was happening. Unmarked and marked cars block the street. The place was crawling in uniformed cops.

"Can you make me look different and hide the bags?"

"That wasn't the task I was sent here to complete."

I sighed audibly. "Can you, or can't you?"

He shrugged, lips tightening in a grimace. "Can't. Not until I've completed my orders from Zeus."

"What's the task?"

"Finally!" Seemingly from thin air, Hermes pulled a clipboard and a pen. "I need your signature. Preferably in blood."

"Not so fast, Hermes." Physically repulsed by the idea of signing a contract in blood, I stepped back. "If my mother was the Oracle, and I inherited her position, why would I need to sign anything?"

The god tapped the clipboard. "Your mother might have been Oracle, and you might have inherited her assets, but that doesn't make you Oracle. You must be chosen and accept the position like any other job. This document says you'll take on the mantle of Oracle to the Gods."

"What's in it for me?" If I could inherit my mom's stuff without being the Oracle and all that it entailed, I would rather do that.

He chuckled, mirth lighting up his whole face. "Good question. One I've never been asked before. How clever of you."

Heat built down low and in my cheeks. "Flattery will get you nowhere. Answer the question. Quickly. Succinctly."

Hermes opened his mouth, cocked his head and then shut it again. With a more earnest expression, he replied, "You will have the benefit of immortality, vigor of youth, and—"

I waved my hands in front of me in a stopping motion. "Wait a second. If immortality is part of the deal, then why isn't there an Oracle right now?"

The god glanced over his shoulder before replying in a low voice, "Nothing is truly immortal. Even gods can be killed."

"Damn. I didn't know that. I thought they were just tossed into Tartarus or something. Gods can die, die?"

"Yes. Some of us are slow." Hermes winked.

I remembered how fast he'd moved when he rescued me from the fire. How he caught me just now. Hermes earned his reputation for speed.

"If I sign, will you help me get out of here?" If I didn't like being Oracle, I could always figure out how to get out of the deal later. There was always a loophole.

A cop noticed us and began his approach, holding up his hand to get our attention. "Hey. Stay where you are!"

Hermes tapped the clipboard. "Only if you sign."

I grabbed the pen and clipboard he practically shoved into my face. The pen pricked my finger, and I felt a pull like a blood draw. When I pressed the pen to the paper, what flowed out as I signed my name was a bit too dark to be red ink.

The cop was still about ten feet away but picking up his pace. Hermes took the pen and clipboard, stowing them away. "Grab your belongings and hold tight, or you'll lose them."

I gripped the handles of everything I owned.

Hermes got behind me in one blink, and in the next, strong arms wrapped around my waist and suddenly the back of me was pressed up against the front of him. The reach around hug was very different than when he'd saved me when I was four. Different, except for the feeling of safety and that I could trust him. I hadn't felt that way since my grandparents died, especially not with Carlo. My erstwhile husband was exciting, not safe.

"Ready?" Hermes' whisper fanned my ear and sent shivers down my neck.

I delighted in the tingling and the fluttering in my gut. "Mmmhmm. So ready."

I was *not* ready for what happened next.

CHAPTER
FIVE

In the 1980s there was a movie called Tron. I saw it at least a billion times. Kid me really liked the special effects and the lasers, etc. Kid me didn't have to feel the effects of going at an ultrafast speed without a car. My body crushed against Hermes's front. The best way to describe the place he took me would be a tunnel, except the darkness of the tunnel seemed to expand infinitely in every direction, as if he carried me through a place that had no up or down. The cold—or rather lack of heat, the absence of gravity, and smell—ozone or something weird—screamed we went somewhere that wasn't Kansas, Toto.

When he finally stopped, I bent over and lost the remainder of my tomato sandwich. He held my hair and rubbed my back making soothing sounds. He offered me a cloth, which I used to wiped the sweat from my forehead and ick from my mouth. None of this was mortifying, at all.

Situated under glaring lights, we ended up in a transit station outside of town. Busses and big rigs pulled in and out. Carlo and I had come to this coastal town to get away from his last scam. Too bad his crew followed, escaping the consequences of the same con.

He'd been truer to those wise guys than his own wife and son. Good thing Luke wasn't dependent on Carlo anymore.

Lifting my gaze, I met Hermes's dark eyes. "Why did you take me to this hellhole?"

"It has many names, but I didn't take you to Hell. Hera's treaty with their king is tentative, and Olympus's herald's presence without notice might be taken as an act of aggression, no matter how brief."

Processing that he was talking about places I'd long ago dismissed as a fabrication, I stammered, "H-hell is real?"

Hermes nodded, taking my gross tissue from my hand and disposing of it. The weird thing about it was I didn't see where the tissue went—it was as if he stuffed it into an invisible pocket.

"As is Hades and the realms within that realm. Very different realms. Very different rulers. King Aidoneus doesn't mind if I flit in and out. Lucifer gets snitty about trespassing."

I snorted. "Lucifer as in the devil aka Satan?"

"He's known by many names by mundanes, but yes, Lucifer is the King of Hell."

"Snitty King of Hell." Shaking my head at the absurdity, I laughed. "Just a year ago you were a figment of my imagination. Now, all this is real and I'm part of it. Okay, let's get going to Washington."

The grin on Hermes' face fell. Something akin to regret filled his deep brown eyes. "I can't take you to Washington, Lydia. I've fulfilled my task and must return to my duties."

Right. I signed the paper. He only assured me that I'd get away from the police. This must be a 'heroine goes it alone' kind of journey. No problem. I'd been together but alone for the past ten years of my twenty-eight-year relationship.

"Okay." I cleared my throat and threw on my polite smile reserved for clients. "Well, goodbye and thanks for the lift here."

Hermes glanced over his shoulder before producing a coin about the size of a silver dollar—except it was gold and appeared real. "If you find yourself in a life-threatening situation, hold this in your hand at a crossroads and think of me."

"A crossroads?"

"An intersection." He pointed to a four-way stop.

"What about a roundabout, do those count?"

Hermes tilted his head to the side, dark eyebrows scrunching together. "What?"

"Never mind."

I was stalling. My stomach had that same ball of dread that had formed and I had carried since the moment he walked away when I was four.

The god was suddenly very close, his heat and the scent of fresh breezes and verdant meadows accompanying him. "If I took you straight to your mother's former dwelling, you would not have the necessary tools to be an oracle. You can't even *see* what's coming yet."

"Yet? When do I get my oracle powers?"

Hermes responded with a cryptic grin, and said, "As the god of roads, I've learned a journey prepares you for many things in life. Make allies, study your enemies, learn all you can about the super-natural world along the way."

The herald of the Olympians took his leave, disappearing into the night.

I opened one of my bags, retrieving a wad of cash from my secret stash. Over the years, I'd hidden a small amount of my earnings in various places around my building, easily retrievable but not places one would look. Once in a while, my stash would get raided by Carlo or one of his low life associates. So, I started breaking it up and getting more creative with my hiding spots.

I had twenty-two hundred dollars stored. Not a lot for a lifetime, but enough to get me across the country and to my house and money there. The neat thing about bus tickets was that you didn't have to provide ID or go through security like in an airport. I bought a ticket to the cheapest city going west in one booth and a ticket up north to

Rochester, New York, not far from the Canadian border in another. If the police somehow tracked me here, they'd see two tickets purchased. Occam's Razor would lead them to the Canadian border. I stood around the station looking to trade someone the Boise, Idaho ticket and some cash for a Seattle ticket.

Just my luck, the next bus to Seattle was in two days.

"I got Denver, Colorado," offered a Black woman in her mid-sixties, judging by her dated clothes and gray locks. "I can always go further and back for some extra money."

Denver was good because it was on the way to Seattle, but a different location from what I'd bought the ticket.

"How much you asking for a trade?"

"Six hundred dollars, to make it worth my time." Her mouth ticked in the corner as she spoke.

Spotting the tell, I held back my grin. "I'll give you three fifty."

"Harrumph. Not worth it."

"A ticket from Boise to Denver is what, eighty to ninety bucks? That gives you a food stipend and a profit."

She arched painted eyebrows. "I'm not the one trying to fool someone." With a pointed look, she added, "Likely the law."

"My husband," I said. It was a half-truth. I didn't want Carlo to know where I was going. "He's a bad man and runs with an even worse crew."

The woman looked into my eyes, saw what she needed and said, "Four hundred, final offer."

I was going to haggle for three seventy-five, but something stopped me. Instead, I touched her hand. My head got all swimmy and weird for a few moments and my vision blurred. When my sight returned to normal, tears stained the woman's cheeks.

"It's true. Every word.," she said, lip quivering. She dabbed at her cheeks with a tissue. "I know it in my marrow."

I cocked my head, unsure of what she meant. Deciding I didn't have time to care, I fumbled with the money, giving her the four hundred she asked for. Finally, we exchanged tickets. My head felt muddled, and exhaustion set in. *It must be the adrenaline wearing off*, I assured myself.

"Best I get going."

Despite feeling weak and sluggish in the head, I managed to get on the bus heading for Denver. With my shop and my marriage behind me, I closed my eyes.

CHAPTER
SIX

Light glaring in my face, I woke in stages. Finally, I peeled my cheek plastered against the bus window. I rubbed the sleep from my eyes and a wiped the drool from my chin with the corner of my other sleeve, taking in my surroundings. My neck screamed with the movement and my entire body felt stiff and achy.

Outside the bus, the land was flat and the sky was broad. Inside, the bus had picked up a lot more passengers than had gotten on at the transit station. I'd slept through at least one stop, if not several. Which meant we'd long since left the sleepy town and my husband Carlo.

An old ache curled in my chest. Avoiding the feeling was the whole reason I didn't get an abortion when I was a teenager and stayed with a two-timing con man so long. My mother left me with that ache. My grandparents did their best to fill the painful void. They loved me well, but had died when I still wasn't ready to face the world alone.

Luke had changed everything. The moment he was born, I no longer felt alone. Children grow up, and if you're lucky, become better people than their parents. A boy scout to the core, Luke didn't like the way his father and I lived, among other beefs between him and his dad, so as soon as he could, my kind child got as far from his charlatan parents as he could. I didn't blame him for distancing himself, but oh, did it leave me lonely. I'd been married to Carlo for eighteen years, at that point, ten years prior to now, but I don't know if he'd ever truly been there.

Knowing that my mother was alive this whole time made the hurt worse.

Why should I serve the gods who made her abandon me? So what if Hermes got me out of a bind twice? He only did it the first time to keep my mom happy, I bet, and the second to get me to sign a damned contract. I knew my Greek myths. He wasn't just a messenger. Hermes was also a trickster. Tricksters didn't give a crap about anyone.

I needed to get out of this Oracle business. The best way I could think of doing that was to not claim my inheritance. If I didn't show, what would the gods do, *make* me serve them? The way I looked at it, they owed me a mother and the kind of childhood that didn't lead me to marrying Carlo. If the Olympians didn't take my mother, I could have had her support and not needed that two-timing piece of dung.

Mind made up, I got off the bus at the Denver terminal. I'd never been this far west before. Judging by the way people openly smiled and looked at each other, there weren't many of my type around here. Good.

Cities were crap for cons. Most people thought cities were great for anonymity and the big barrel of fish. Most people were idiots.

Big city dwellers had a kind of savvy about hustlers that developed early. If people ran games on you since elementary school: dealers trying to get you hooked, the guy bumming money and never paying back, the other poor kids stealing your shoes, you tended to be world weary and wizened up by time you were an adult.

Small towns weren't my thing either. Most people in small towns had lived their whole lives there. Their entire family had done the same for generations. The community ties ran deep. They wouldn't trust newcomers with their future.

I needed something mid-sized to smallish town, with about ten to twenty thousand people. Big enough that I could have plenty of fish, yet small enough that they had a bit of trust in their new neighbor.

I dragged my suitcases through the people milling about and found my way to the posted bus schedule. I picked a place and bought a ticket with cash.

Now, the city might not be a place to set up permanently, but a bus station was filled with hopefuls. Here, I could make a quick buck to start my new life.

With three hours to kill before my bus departed, I set up the suitcases as a makeshift table and sat on a chair provided for waiting passengers. Then I spread a cloth out, attached a sign that read, "Tarot Readings: $5" and brought out a mason jar painted with sun, moon, and stars. Once I set that up, I shuffled a tarot deck and laid out a spread. If you look for a client, they won't think they need to look for you.

Within minutes I got my first customer. Judging by a few streaks of grey in her sandy hair and her mild laugh lines and crow's feet, a woman in her late thirties, maybe early forties approached. From her thin frame hung a shapeless sundress that was faded enough from laundering for me to know it wasn't new but was likely one of her best or favorite outfits. The sandals on her feet had seen better days.

If I weren't in dire straits, I wouldn't take a penny from her until I could help her more. Set up for real somewhere, I could lead her to a better job, get her some extra income, or lead her to a shopaholic friend who loved to give away their unworn castoffs, so their husband didn't find out how much they spent on something they didn't even want. I was good at connecting my clients to help build a community.

Something slithered in my chest, curled around my heart, and squeezed.

Starting over sucked.

The stranger counted out five ones and shoved them in my direction.

In turn, I cast my eyes to the makeshift table. "Set it there," I said, laying on my grandmother's Greek accent thickly upon each word. "If you're not satisfied with my reading, you may take it with you."

Her eyes widened and her hand touched her chest. "Seriously?"

A knot of guilt twisted in my stomach. This woman hadn't caught a break in a long, long time. I forced a smile. "Of course, my dear."

It was easy to tell what she wanted to know. The same thing most people wanted to hear, health and safety for themselves and loved ones, financial security, and any current problem will be solved just around the corner.

"Would you like a general reading, or a three card draw?"

She worried at her lip, clutching the cash to her stomach. If money troubles weren't already apparent from sizing her up, she gave it away then. "What's the difference?"

"A general offers a little more insight into your life in general. A three-card draw will answer a specific question." I hoped she'd ask for a three card draw, it was quick and usually easy to answer. I'd need a longer rapport to give her a general reading that wasn't so ambiguous that it could apply to anyone yet didn't fit the answer she sought. She'd likely be dissatisfied and would either give me the cash out of pride or walk away with the money and tell everyone that I'm a scam artist.

"A three card draw?"

I placed the tarot cards on the table in a neat pile, then gestured to that pile. "Take the cards and give them a shuffle with a question in your mind."

The blonde did as I instructed, tentatively, as if sweeping for landmines instead of picking up and shuffling a deck of cards.

I held out my hand as if she'd done it for a prescribed amount of time, but I simply wanted to turn this client around and snag another. I had a whole life to start over in Colorado. I'd need more than my puny nest egg to establish myself with a new setup.

Our fingers brushed.

A fuzzy sensation bloomed in my head like cotton. Colors swirled before me. The chatter, the overhead speaker, the shuffle of feet, and distant music of a busker muffled.

No, no, no! Whatever this newfound illness was, I couldn't afford for it to happen now. I shook my head, my vision clearing and hearing returning with the movement.

The woman in a sundress was gone.

A man in uniform stood in her place. He was in his late twenties and smelled of the same aftershave my son Luke used.

"Ma'am, you can't do that here without a license." He gestured to my setup and then regarded me with kind brown eyes so much like my son's peepers, it hurt to look at him.

I cleared my throat. "Oh, sorry officer. I'm new here. This was fine in Philly." I hadn't ever lived in Philadelphia, but judging by the local coloring of his accent, he hadn't ever been there either, let alone knew the laws.

He smiled a small, warm smile. "Welcome to Denver, but you got to have a license to solicit, okay?"

Gaze on the milling crowd, I nodded absently, wondering where the woman went. I hated that I'd lost five dollars because I had some sort of mental fog. I wondered if this had something to do with going through menopause, or if I was losing my mind. Maybe I imagined Hermes, the blood signature, and Dione. Maybe Carlo leaving me after all these years caused me to have a mental breakdown instead of a midlife crisis. It wasn't as if someone like me could see a doctor.

"I'll let you keep your current profits, but you got to pack up, ma'am."

Unsure if I heard him correctly, I tilted my head to the side. "Profits?"

The officer pointed to the overflowing cash jar and the pile of bills around it. "That's a lot of cash, ma'am. You should put it some-where out of sight."

I stared at the money. I'd lost time. A lot of time. "What time is it?"

His forehead wrinkled. "It's half-past eight p.m. ma'am. Do you have a bus to catch?"

Two hours ago.

I wasn't going to admit I'd lost most of the day. I shook my head and collected the cash. There weren't just fivers. I spotted tens, twen-ties and more than one Benjamin Franklin in there. "No. It leaves tomorrow," I lied. "Do you know of a clean, safe, and inexpensive hotel nearby?"

CHAPTER

SEVEN

The cop directed me to a motel that suited my needs. It was clean, but cheap and in a less-than-desirable neighborhood. Most importantly, the cheerful clerk at the front desk assured me the room had two deadbolts on the door.

The flat screen television played ads for Colorado tourism destinations—a woman blabbing on about the Colorado river and its legends. The motor of the minifridge hummed louder than necessary, but I liked the white noise. The television, fridge, and the distant grinding and clinking of an ice machine soothed my nerves.

Carlo and I had spent a good chunk of our early marriage in motel rooms like this. Those days had been fun, when life seemed like an adventure.

In front of me, over two thousand dollars was freshly counted and stacked in neat piles on the hotel bed. This also felt familiar. Instead of Carlo winning it big at some race, I had earned the money with whatever came out of my mouth while I was out of it.

Getting a solicitor's license and setting up shop in the bus station wouldn't be bad, if I could shove aside that I lost awareness of time and place for hours, that is. Nothing like that had ever happened to me before.

Did the blood signature give me the gift of visions under certain conditions? I didn't like not having control of it or anyone to ask.

My yayá, Marina, recounted tales of Oracles at Apollo's temple on Mount Delphi, sitting on a tripod chair, inhaling the noxious vapors from a stream that channeled along the floor in a manmade ravine, and munching on laurel leaves to achieve an altered state to receive their prophetic visions. The combination was very important to receive prophetic visions, she'd said. She'd said nothing about losing time.

I'd popped some ibuprofen and had sat on public seating inhaling the noxious fumes of bus exhaust, not exactly the same. However, that meant I could only have some control over the visions. The notion of not being aware of my surroundings, vulnerable to any sort of attack, didn't sit right with me. I'd been surviving by having my wits about me way too long.

"What's the use of being an oracle if I can't use it to my advantage?" I threw up my hands and fell backwards onto the pillows, dramatically tossing an arm over my forehead.

Instead of wallowing in self-pity, I sat up and rolled the piles of cash. After securing them with rubber bands, I hid the rolls in a secret compartment of the suitcase with all my grandparents' stuff. Anyone who opened the suitcase would think it was worthless family memorabilia and toss it. Young thieves didn't have the imagination nor the curiosity of the older generations. They looked for pricey electronics or things that could be easily sold at a pawn shop.

I would figure being an oracle out. I just needed to sleep on it.

Closing my eyes, I let exhaustion consume me once again.

I dreamt of mountains so green and skies of a dull gray, and of an older place. A place with sturdy columns and marble walls. A place where women wore chitons, statues came to life, monsters were pets, and my grandparents' worthless belongings were objects of power.

"Lydia," a smokey voice called in a dulcet tone.

I rolled over, mumbling a Greek curse my grandfather used to use when he thought I wasn't listening. Carlo knew what it meant and would know to leave me alone.

"Lydia!"

I rubbed my eyes and sat up, rubbing my eyes again at what I saw.

Dione was on the television, hands on her hips, and a disappointed look on her face. "Watch your tongue or you'll lose it."

"Signomi," I replied wearily.

Dione flicked her wrist. "No apologies. I need you to pack your things and continue your journey. It isn't safe for you to stay unguarded and fall into a trance. Don't fly. Hera reigns in the sky."

"What's Hera have to with anything?"

Dione grimaced. "The queen's loyalties are in question."

"Loyalty to whom?"

"*Me*. Get on a bus or a train and get to the Olympics in Washington. On the way there you can read up on a device about our family history."

I touched my chest. "Our family history? I'm the granddaughter of a sheep herder and a weaver." They'd become restauranteurs when they immigrated to the U.S. If Dione knew my mother, then she knew the story.

"Those were occupations held by gods in Olympus, my dear. Once you are safely on your way, search for how Zeus came into power. I think it's happening again."

I knew how Zeus had come into power, but I didn't want to talk about that. I was still stuck on "our family history."

"Are we related?"

Dione looked behind her, worry limning her beautiful face. The television flickered. An ad about rafting resumed as if she'd never been there at all.

I rubbed my temples, unsure if I'd seen Dione or if I'd hallucinated the whole interaction. Maybe I couldn't handle Carlo leaving, and I'd lost it. Was this whole thing a midlife crisis, or a mental break of some sort?

Just as I was about to dismiss the occurrence to my fragile mind, something rustled under the blanket at the foot of the bed. Fearing a mouse, I squeaked and rapidly sprang to my feet. The shape was all wrong for a mouse, long and slender like a—*no, no, no*! I hopped onto the nightstand, balancing precariously.

I'm glad my first instinct wasn't to jump on the floor. Movement there caught my attention. Writhing bodies of snakes too numerous to count carpeted the floor.

This had been a reoccurring nightmare since I'd watched Indiana Jones. I only had to avoid them long enough until I could wake from this terrible dream. I pinched myself, hoping to wake. Instead, I yelped when my nails bit into my skin.

Panic rivaled with the overwhelming thought that if I was awake this was all a delusion.

If I stepped down onto the floor, all the snakes would disappear, and I'd feel like an idiot, a committable idiot. Instead of dipping my foot, I pulled the pillow from the bed with the snakes—yes, there were plural there now—under the covers. I dropped the pillow, the snakes cleared.

With a deep breath, I grabbed my bag hanging from the headboard and I jumped, landing near my suitcases next to the door. I swung my big ol' mom bag at the serpents with one hand and barricaded myself from the slithering mass with my suitcases. This bought me time to open the door. Thankfully, no snakes lurked outside. I dragged the suitcases and swung the purse, until I could get the door shut.

I slumped against a car, catching my breath.

A very idiotic part of my brain wanted to open the door to see if I was hallucinating before. The intelligent part of me said it didn't matter if they were real or not, I needed to get the heck out of Denver. If they were real, I was in danger of finding out what kind of supernatural could get a myriad of snakes in a motel room. If I was losing it, Lukie would get me good psychiatric care once I reached Washington.

However, if the snakes were real, housekeeping was in for a surprise.

I grabbed an old receipt and a pen from my purse, then wrote, "Vermin inside. Call animal control."

I slipped the note into the crack of the door and admired my work for about 3 seconds. There. Vagueness didn't give away my crazy.

Deciding not to look back, I carried one suitcase and rolled the other to the office. The din of traffic soothed me into a sense of normalcy. When I got to the counter, the cheerful clerk from earlier in the evening was gone, replaced by a man with stringy hair, mostly covered by a trucker hat. Grease stains marred a faded 80s Kiss concert t-shirt draped on his wiry frame. While eyeing me like I was a problem he didn't want to deal with, he wiped something questionably mud colored from his fingers with a paper napkin. The person earlier had on khakis and a polo shirt with a name tag.

The motel got really informal on night shift, I supposed.

The way he eyed me telegraphed he was trying to creep me out enough to take my questions elsewhere.

I'd just faced a squirming myriad of venomous snakes. I wasn't afraid of discount Honky-tonk Hank. "What time is the next shuttle to the bus station?"

"Ain't one."

I wanted to argue that I took one here, but then remembered it was a city bus. I didn't want to wait alone in the dark in an unfamiliar city for a bus on an iffy schedule. Especially after Dione's warning and what just happened in my room.

I had a little money to splurge on a rideshare.

"I need a Ridebuddy to the bus station."

"Okay."

"I need you to contact them."

"Don't got the app?"

Why would I bother with you, dumbass, if I had it? After taking a deep breath, I replied, "No. I lost my cell phone."

He eyed me for a second like I was the stupidest person he'd ever seen. Given the way he looked and acted, that really hurt my ego. "You need an app for Ridebuddy."

I pinched the bridge of my nose. "Do cabs exist out here?"

He scowled. "'Course. Denver's a big city."

I gave him an expectant look. When I got nothing but a blank stare and open mouth breathing in reply, I gestured to the phone on the counter. "Will you call me a cab, please?"

The "please" I added on noticeably later than the request. Normally, I didn't get frustrated with customer service employees, but he rubbed me the wrong way. Not to mention I had a room *filled with snakes!*

"Be my guest." He turned the phone to face me and pivoted away, leaving me for whatever he had going on the back.

I did *not* want to know.

I dialed "0" hoping operators still existed. It didn't work. I tried 411. Still nothing. I'd been dependent on cell phones and the internet for information for so long, I didn't know what to do.

Then I noticed the business cards stacked on a little case. One was for a taxi service. The rest were all cards for private drivers who worked for rideshares.

"You need an app," I mumbled, rifling through the cards. It didn't take long to arrange for a car to come pick me up. The driver knew the hotel and said they could be there in fifteen minutes. We had a bad connection, and they had an unfamiliar accent, so I hoped that's what they'd said.

I hung up and didn't call out to thank the clerk since he hadn't been much help anyway. I hoped housekeeping would see my note. I hadn't even told the clerk. If it was a delusion, he might call some authority to take me away.

To my surprise, a car was already there waiting for me. The dashboard had the Ridebuddy lighted sign. The driver wore sunglasses, and a gator covered their face—some people still liked to wear masks if they had to deal with public, so I thought nothing of it. They had long dreads and looked feminine-ish.

I knocked on the window just in case. "Are you Jen?"

The driver nodded once and popped the trunk. Jen wasn't a full-service cab, obviously. That was fine by me. I could lug my own bags.

After I loaded my suitcases, I got in the backseat. Adrenaline waning, I didn't think it would hurt to rest my eyes. Besides, arriving at the bus terminal would take a while.

CHAPTER

EIGHT

*S*everal women dressed in white chitons waited in line before me. Most of them were dark-haired and young. They sang songs and one played a tiny harp—a lyre maybe? The words they sang were in Greek, sort of, I didn't understand all the words.

Odd. I'm fluent in Greek. My grandparents preferred it around the house and at their restaurant whenever they weren't serving patrons. Why was I not catching as many words as I should?

Dione, or a younger version of her, greeted us, leading us all to a marble temple. I waved, or rather, I wanted to wave. My body seemed to have a mind of its own.

Just past Dione, a gorgeous dude with curling salt and pepper hair and dark olive skin, lounged on a dais. The guy had nothing on.

Usually, I'd avert my eyes—no unsolicited "D" view, thank you very much—but I couldn't look away.

One of the women in a white chiton, belted at the waist, approached the dais.

The hunk boy eyed her with unabashed lust. A smile curved his sensuous lips.

He was handsome but so freaking typical.

46

The woman pulled up her chiton to her waist and straddled him.

If these women were lining up to ride the dude, I wanted O.U.T. No way was I going to be joystick user number thirty-two. I turned, seeking a space to flee.

Mountains and a valley below offered refuge.

A hand gripped my shoulder. Someone said something in that not-quite-Greek. My brain translated it as, "We need him. He holds the key to freeing them."

My own snore chain-sawed through my dream, tearing me away from the gross scene. It took me a moment to figure out where I was and when I was. I had the distinct feeling that I'd seen something from the past, but then again, I was seeing a lot of stuff that didn't make much sense.

Through bleary eyes, I looked out Jen's car window, expecting to see Denver's flat cityscape at night. Instead, we were surrounded by mountains with low brush and bare-faced rocks, and it was daytime

I cleared my throat. "Where are you taking me?"

Jen turned her head all the way around. The gator fell away from her face with the movement, revealing a human-ish woman with green-gold scales instead of skin. Her lips parted, exposing long, thin fangs.

Ice water flowed through my veins as my stomach bottomed out. I fought with the handle of the door, desperate to escape the monster.

"The key is safe," she-it assured me, speaking in Greek. Her voice was sibilant and inhuman as heck, only adding to my fear. Her head spun back to face where she was driving. What I'd mistaken as dreads the night before were snakes. They wriggled to life, dancing in front of my face like a viper chorus.

"Oh, Hell no."

At least that's what I'd meant to say. My voice came out a shriek as I backed against the rear passenger door.

Jen-monster cried out. The vipers hissed and recoiled from my voice. Still, I continued to scream. How the heck else was I supposed to react to a reptile lady with snake hair?

The car veered off the road into a ditch. The driver door flung open, and Jen-monster couldn't get out fast enough.

I crawled over the seat. More like I flung myself awkwardly, getting stuck halfway, my backside unable to squeeze through the tight space. Somehow, I managed to wriggle free, ending up in the driver's seat. It reeked of some sort of musky oil.

Ew.

No time to be grossed out by stinky odors, I slammed the door shut and got the car in gear. The wheels spun for a second, kicking up reddish dirt, but the front wheel drive pulled through and got me back on the highway.

When you're in a situation like this, the best thing to do is to look forward and get away. I, however, don't always do the best thing and glanced in the rearview mirror.

What I saw would haunt my nightmares for a long time to come.

Jen-monster had a somewhat human head and torso, but instead of hips and legs she had a snake body, split into two-scaled tails. Those tails propelled her toward the car at an alarming rate.

I stomped my foot on the gas, but the vehicle was slow to make up its mind and shift to a faster gear.

In one of his many ventures into the criminal underworld, Carlo and his crew used to steal cars and chop them for parts. I wasn't supposed to know the cars were stolen, but the chop shop was a place I'd spent some time. I cursed when I realized the car had great horsepower but little torque. Finally, the engine caught on, careening down the road.

My damn eyes betrayed me, glancing once again in the rearview mirror. Jen-monster wasn't as close, but she was gaining ground. I swore. How the heck was the giant snake-woman moving so fast?

Eyes once again ahead, ominous, charcoal clouds churned into the bright, blue sky, darkness swathing the vista like a blanket.

Thunder rumbled and a bolt of lightning struck the road ahead, its flash almost blinding.

I squinted, not because of the flash. Something appeared in the road where the lightning had hit. That something grew larger and larger.

"What the fu—"

At first, the creature seemed like a dragon with massive leather wings spread behind a human-ish torso. The thing had to be ten or twenty stories high for me to even see it at this distance. The shoulders bore a hundred or more snake heads. A giant head resembling some mix of a lion, bear, and dragon stuck out a forked tongue. Pleasant. Snakes crawled along the torso and extended from the monster's arms instead of hands. He-it had a similar bottom half to Jen-monster with a split serpent tail for legs.

Laughter bubbled up. "Fantastic! A matching pair!"

The storm seemed to swirl and eddy along with the monster's movements. Rain beat down in torrential sheets everywhere else.

Panic seized my chest, but I could still think. With the most terrifying thing I'd ever seen in front of me and Jen-monster in the back, I had very few options except for which monster did I let eat me first. Maybe they'd go at each other, fighting over their prey like Godzilla and Mothra. A nice clash of titans while I escaped.

The storm-snake-dragon-man-thing breathed fire out of one of its heads and the rest of them made sounds an awful lot like a lion's roar, a bark, a howl, and a chorus of wildlife noises at once.

I shook my head. "Nope. Not a hallucination. That's just freaking weird."

I needed a plan. Perhaps I could try to off-road it in a midsized sedan? I pictured myself running into a bush and totaling the car and my one chance of escape shot.

Somebody was on my side, because just then I spotted a dirt road and veered onto it, tires kicking up dirt on the turn. I floored it.

In my rearview, the storm-snake-thing and Jen-monster

appeared. I hoped they were going to fight over their prey. No such luck. The freakish monsters joined forces in their pursuit.

Aw! Snakey people sticking together warmed my heart, proving anyone could find true love...except me. I laughed. I had to. If I didn't, I'd curl up in a ball and die.

The rain came steadily down. Lightning blazed through the sky striking precariously close to the car. I didn't need to look in the rearview to know that they were gaining on me.

Part of me wished this was all a dream. Another part slapped that part. I may've been in the sites of monsters but at least I wasn't dying the slow death of being trapped in a bad marriage. Every turn I made was my decision. Every bit of money I earned stayed mine. Every mistake was mine to make. I didn't have to make up for Carlo's crap anymore either. I was free!

A massive snake tail shot past and then coiled around the car. Metal groaned and creaked as it crumpled. My stomach plummeted as the entire vehicle rose from the ground.

I was free of my bad marriage, yes, but I was going to die before I got to enjoy that freedom.

CHAPTER

NINE

Instead of crushing the car, Snakeman coiled the vehicle in his right tail and dragged it through the Colorado wilderness—mostly low brush and dirt. The view of the two serpent monsters of disparate sizes holding hands—or rather the abhorrent appendages that served as hands—would be touching if I weren't cold-sweating with panic over how long I had to live.

Would they suck the meat off my bones over a nice candlelit table, washing down each bite with my exsanguinated blood served in fine crystal goblets? At least my death would be more romantic than my life—not for me, but that tracks, too.

A small, circular object gleamed in the passenger seat, catching my eye. Hermes' coin somehow made its way out of my purse in the back into my field of vision. Interesting. Snatching the coin, I slid it into my bra and out of sight. There wasn't a crossroads here, but maybe I could escape and find one, eventually.

Just when I'd mustered a seed of hope that I'd get to Hermes, the terrain changed. The car and loving couple sank, dragging the car into what appeared to be a lake. Murky water gurgled all around, enveloping the vehicle. Enveloping wasn't the right word. There seemed to be about an arms-length of empty air between the window and the water.

How touching! The monster sweethearts made a bubble around me.

I had plenty of air, but my brain went into full panic mode. Because if I wasn't panicking, I wouldn't have tried the door. Maybe later I'd be grateful the handle didn't work and kick myself for trying. For now, I would hyperventilate.

The intersection where I'd turned onto the dirt road popped in my head. If I could escape and get there, I could get to Hermes. Fat chance. We were so deep underwater; I could no longer see my hands in front of my face. Wan light eventually seeped in.

My skin tingled as we passed through an invisible barrier which separated the lake from what appeared to be an enormous cave. As if a forcefield holding me in place broke, I slammed against the ceiling of the car, bumping my head. It took me a second to adjust to my new position and look out the driver's side window to take in my surroundings.

Most of it was a distant rock wall, green and brown like oxidized copper. The car zigzagged as it scraped against the cavern floor beneath the roof. The floor studded with random stalagmites, occasionally blocking my view.

Stalactites far above glowed greenish yellow, providing an eerie light. The metal of the car scraped against rock until it stopped moving.

The tail slipped away.

The major dilemma I now faced was that I was once again in danger of being devoured, or at the very least, gruesomely murdered.

My heart pummeled my ribs. I had a hard time thinking straight through the fear.

C'mon Lydia. You've been in a tight spot before. They might be monsters, but this isn't a movie. They want something from me. If I figured out their hustle, I could get away. I'd faced an enemy or two of Carlo's before. Thinking that the monsters were like shady hustlers helped, I could relax and think of my counter-hustle.

If the monsters wanted me dead, they wouldn't have gone to the trouble of bringing me down here. The snakes were a tactic to get me out of my room, away from people and into Jen's car. That meant the heinous-looking couple didn't like their business public. They wanted to ransom me or make their own deal. I could work with that. Or rather, pretend to work with that. Nobody on the up and up liked to make deals in dim, underwater caves.

The passenger window smashed open, glass shattering behind me. The door screeched, ripped from the hinges by the same scaled tail that smashed the glass.

I backed against the driver door, avoiding the probing tail. "I'll come out, but you got to let me do it on my own." I took a chance these monsters didn't know English and spoke in Greek.

The tail slithered away.

Okay. Deal time.

CHAPTER

TEN

After an ordeal of climbing out of a glass-riddled, upside-down car, one would think facing monsters would be no big deal, but it was. It *really* was. Jen had almost a Predator aesthetic going on, but her big ol' partner was a far cry scarier—not to mention plain-out more gross—than anything a modern horror writer could come up with.

I racked my brain to come up with who they might be from Greek mythology, or should I say Greek History, since all those bedtime stories my grandparents told were apparently real.

Jen was the spokesperson of the two. "I told you, the key is safe. No harm to the key."

At least, that's what I gleaned from what she'd said. She spoke in a Greek dialect of some sort. Maybe it was ancient Greek? I didn't know.

"If by key, you mean me. You and I have very different definitions of what no harm means." I swept my hand down the length of my body, indicating my cuts, bruises, and other evidence of definite *harm.*

The snakes on Jen's head writhed and hissed. Her partner's tails snapped behind him. Animal noises of dissent bellowed from all the heads on his shoulders.

I cringed. Maybe I shouldn't have come into this negotiation with complaints.

Jen smiled a viper's smile, mouth stretching too far to be human. She said in what was mostly modern Greek. "Key run. We catch."

"Understood." My voice cracked on the word.

At the tilt of her head, I repeated myself in modern Greek. She still seemed to not quite understand the word but got the gist. How could she have not have adapted? Dione was ancient, older than most Olympians, but still spoke like a modern person.

I guess if a supernatural didn't have a human appearance, they didn't bother trying to assimilate into the human world. I could be wrong though. It was best not to assume anything except I needed to get out of here. I cut to the chase.

"What do you want from me?"

"Key." Jen gestured to follow her, showing me to a recess in the cavern. She then indicated for me to stand in the recess.

"I still don't know what you want. Can we make a bargain?"

The monster shook her head. "No bargain. Key remains here. Safe here."

To emphasize her point, snakes slithered from her head down her body to the floor. More snakes slithered from who knows where, joining them. They wove together creating a hideous, writhing curtain.

I sighed. *So much for wheeling and dealing my way out of here.*

With nothing else to do but wait, I took stock of my injuries. Most of the cuts on my hands had healed. Also, the bruising had gone from deep purple to yellowing, as if days had passed. Given I was somewhere that didn't feel quite like Colorado, or Earth for that matter, perhaps it had been days. Or maybe this was part of the excellent health Hermes told me about.

I pulled the coin from my bra, rubbing it between my fingers and thinking of Hermes. Nothing. Sighing, I put the coin back. Of course,

I couldn't depend on someone to help me. When had anyone ever come to my rescue? There was no intersection here, and I'd been on my own for the last twenty-eight years, anyway.

Beyond the Curtain of Terror, shouts rang out, echoing through the cavern. No, not shouts. Women shrieking at the top of their lungs —a shield-maiden war cry like on that historically inaccurate, but oh so good, Raiders of the Middle Ages, a TV show Carlo and I used to watch. Barks, roars, hisses and all kinds of Animal Kingdom nonsense countered the cries.

A battle ensued...and I couldn't see any of it.

I stepped back in the nook, crouched and chewed on my finger-nails, not knowing who to root for. The current captors hadn't harmed me. Better the devil you know had been my policy with Carlo. I deluded myself for years that if I stayed with my now-estranged husband, there was no chance of him leaving or of me getting my heartbroken.

Except my theory had been wrong. I'd let him abuse my trust and the vows of our marriage because I was afraid of change. Maybe whoever was out there meant to free me. I allowed myself a modicum of hope in a hopeless situation.

A clear and heartbreakingly beautiful voice rose out of the cacophony.

Compelled to get closer to the voice, I rose to my feet. The hissing curtain of snakes pissed me off. They stood between me and that gorgeous voice. I could have it all. True love, riches, anything could be mine if only I could get to that *voice*!

Anger welled inside me, hot and fierce. My fingers tingled as I raised my arms. A bolt of lightning shot from my fingertips, frying the snakes. An inhuman scream echoed the dying sounds of the serpents. The blackened ash crumbled.

I've never hurt a thing in my life, but at the moment, I didn't care about the pain I may have caused Jen or the stupid snakes. I had to get to that voice.

"What the heck is that, Miriam?" a tan woman with brown hair asked a monster with pink hair, white antlers, paper-white skin, and glowing eyes the color of green glass. Both women were pretty, but the latter was beautiful in an otherworldly way. Like Dione. Like Hermes.

A third young woman, with fire engine red braids, and light brown skin stood with them. Dark eyes that seemed older than the stars scanned their surroundings. She was something very old in young woman's body.

I recognized them all from the viral videos about supernaturals. The pink-haired one had been on the Jenna Jones talk show.

The antlered monster's faced scrunched up. "Demigod...and something else. Never seen that color before." To me she said, "My name is Miriam. I represent covenless witches and high fae in the Supernatural Council of the Americas."

I didn't care who she was or what she represented. All that mattered was the voice. I raised my hand. They were in my way of that voice. "Move!"

I didn't recognize the sound coming from me. It was resonant. Powerful.

Miriam held up their hands, backing up and saying to the others, "The siren song has her spellbound."

"Faerie?" The younger woman asked.

The antlered one nodded and then shouted, "Fear! Fear!"

I had no idea what they were on about. It didn't matter what they said. All that mattered was that sweet, sweet promise. Monsters of all sorts: a werewolf, three angels, a giant lizard, a hairy Sasquatch, all crowded Jen and Snake monster guy.

Women with rainbow-hued feathers and Spartan-looking armor flew in a circle around them all. The most beautiful hovered, singing.

The monsters who kidnapped me looked like pythons entranced by a snake charmer, swaying to her voice. She was for *me*. Lightning crackled between my fingertips, forming into a giant bolt in my grasp.

A horned man with bronze skin got in my way, tossing me a panty-melting smile. "Not so fast, child of Olympus."

He dragged me through cold water that wasn't wet. Vertigo swept my brain up in a whirlwind. My stomach flipped. I couldn't tell right from left, up from down. Then we were in Heaven.

ELEVEN

pparently, in Heaven they serve tea and snacks. I sipped from a porcelain cup which had tiny figures dancing around the rim like an animated gif. Normally, I would be amazed by the magical teacup, but right now, I was busy watching the monsters gather outside the cozy cottage.

Prince Phyr, *"not fear,"* sat across from me inside, gaze flicking between me and the goings on outside. Mostly he watched the fae princess, Miriam. I knew that look. I'd once had eyes for Carlo like that.

Besides Hermes, Phyr might be one of the most gorgeous people I'd ever seen. Fine angles to his face, bright amber eyes, skin like burnished bronze, and black hair that looked like spun silk.

It wasn't just the fae prince. Everyone outside was extraordinarily good looking. What the heck was up with that? Must be a supernatural thing.

Then again, I might not be all human either. I stared at my fingers. I didn't look like them though. I looked like a middle-aged mom—greying dark hair and lines around my eyes and mouth. Still, I made lightning bolts come out my fingers. That zapping power would've come in handy when I was in the car. I don't know if I could've harmed Jen though. She scared me, but she didn't hurt me. Not on purpose, anyway.

A short, possibly Latinx or Mediterranean woman entered the cottage. She was the athletic version of me. Curly dark hair with some grays, brown eyes, and olive complexion. She wore the Spartanesque uniform of the sirens. Could sirens look human or was she some sort of goddess in charge of them?

Heat flooded my face when I remembered the way I reacted when she was in siren form. I hoped I wasn't facing Persephone. Her judgments were swift and wrathful.

"Is Jen alright?" I asked. "I didn't mean to fry her snakes."

The woman ignored me. Her eyes were on the handsome and charming Phyr. She nudged her head toward the door. "Give us a minute."

Phyr rose and then sketched a bow to me, like a courtier in a historical fantasy. "I hope you learn the truth and your power protects you, lovely Lydia."

His words had a magic to them. His hope, a charm. Wow. A real live faerie prince gave me a bit of his luck. Nice.

I needed it.

The newcomer, maybe siren/maybe goddess sat at the table opposite of me. She asked in Greek, "How did you end up in the mouth of Tartarus?"

Instead of answering this woman, I asked, "Who the heck are you that I should tell you anything?"

"My name is Lucinda. I serve the goddess Persephone as ambassador to Earth and as a re-activated general in her siren army." I could hear the reticence of accepting the latter post in her tone. This siren had someone, perhaps a family back on Earth, she didn't want to leave,

I wondered if she could be an ally until she finished with the sentence, "You have Olympian blood. No Olympian can set foot in Hades without express permission of King Adonieus or Queen Persephone. Treaty was broken. That could lead to war. I need to know whether you meant to be there or not to diffuse the situation. Help me, please."

I rubbed my head. Of course, oracles had Olympian blood, including me. The gods were always getting busy with some pretty earthly priestess or another. I wasn't one to spill my personal tea, but I didn't want to cause a war between Olympus and the Underworld over something that wasn't my fault. However, it was the please that finally won me over.

"I was on my way to Washington to serve as the new Oracle. I thought Jen was a RideBuddy driver, not a monster. When I saw what she really was, I stole her car and tried to get away. That's when the other monster jumped in and the two dragged me to... wherever that was. I did *not* go willingly."

Lucinda nodded along, listening to my every word intently. She kept her expression neutral. I sounded like a delusional weirdo, but she took it all in as if she heard this kind of thing every day. What a life a siren must have!

When I finished, she said with a rueful smile, "My condolences about your mother. What happened to Apollonia was a shame. She was a friend of mine. Thanks to your testimony we have a better idea of who was responsible for her death. You're lucky we got there when we did. Typhon and Echidna escaped Tartarus for a reason, and I think it's you."

I gasped, "Typhon and Echidna?"

I'd been kidnapped by two notorious Titans. Their physical appearance should've been a big clue, but it's one thing to have your grandparents teach you Greek mythology as childhood bedtime stories, and quite another to face the monsters of those stories as a middle-aged adult.

"The monsters killed my mother?" Rage ignited within me. I looked at my hands, no sparks. Futile anger boiled inside with no means to discharge it form my body.

"You'll have no power here unless Miriam says so. We're in her faerie, not a normal reality," Lucinda explained.

I nodded. Phyr had already explained that faeries were pocket universes and that the rules depended on the belief of the High Fae who created the faerie. I hadn't heard shield-maidens. I'd heard the ban sidhe cry of the Mórrígan.

Titans were so freaking powerful, it took a Celtic goddess reincarnated, a nephil, an angel, a Hawaiian demigoddess, fae, shifters, a Bigfoot, and a group of sirens to lure them into a faerie prison. They would await there until Persephone and Aidoneus decided what to do with Titans who knew how to escape Tartarus.

"I'm an oracle to the gods, in a faerie of a high fae princess because two Titans wanted to kidnap me. This is definitely not reality."

"If it helps, I don't know if Echidna and Typhon meant to kill your mother. Oracles are special because they have human, Titan, and Olympian blood. They can see through the multiverse and pick a future in the skein laid out by the fates. Once the Oracle sees a future, the other threads are snipped."

Clotho, Lachesis, and Atropos—the Morai— were the three fates. Greeks loved their weaving metaphors. Especially my grandmother, an Arachova-born weaver. She told me Clotho spun the threads of a human's life while we were still developing in the womb. All our major choices and consequences of those choices become a tapestry of sorts. Lachesis would determine the length of the threads or the span of a mortal's life. Atropos would set the point where she would cut the human's life. She was unbendable in this decision. When Atropos said your time was up, there was no bargaining for more. However, this was for mortals, not the gods.

I clasped my hands together so the siren wouldn't see me shake. "They wanted me to see the future of all mortals. Did they want me to see Atropos's final cut?"

Lucinda placed a comforting hand over mine and then said in lightly Spanish-accented English, "Oh, nena. That's only a guess.

You're the one who possesses the gift. You know how it works better than I do."

My lips spread in a weary smile. I had no clue how my oracle gift worked, only the formula to bring on a vision—and that was an educated guess. However, I didn't think my life would mean very much if I admitted that.

CHAPTER

TWELVE

"I have to report to my queen," Lucinda announced, rising. "My friends will see you home."

Home. An interesting concept, considering I didn't have one yet, only a promised property upon arrival. I stood up. "I have luggage in the car. There's priceless family heirlooms in them."

The siren's mouth twisted; her expression pensive as if considering what she would do about it. Some internal decision made; she nodded her head curtly.

"Phyr can retrieve your things."

"It's my stuff. How would he—"

She waved her hands, interrupting me. "You can't go back to the Underworld, at least not so close to Tartarus. It's for your own safety. We don't know what exactly the Titans planned to do with you there."

I wanted to argue, but it seemed like a good plan to me. I followed Lucinda out of the cottage. There was a group standing nearby. A willowy blonde, a dark-haired woman with eyes that reminded me of a predator in the wild, a tall woman with spiral curls, who waved and smiled, a red-haired man who was a little shorter than average holding her hand, and a man that resembled that one movie star and a taller ginger. They were the supernaturals on the viral video. Except, they weren't the strangest thing around.

"Curiouser and curiouser," I whispered, feeling a lot like I'd fallen down the rabbit hole.

"Faeries are freaking weird," replied a woman with brown hair leaning against the cottage.

I recognized her as the woman who was with Miriam and the younger woman earlier. Next to her were two men, one tall and blonde and big, the other of average height with long, thin dreads pulled back in a ponytail. They stopped their conversation to look in my direction. Both had a wary expression, and both seemed to want me to not look at the woman who spoke.

I had no problem forgetting about her.

When I was in the Underworld, it felt like a cavern on earth. The glowing stalactites should have been my first clue something was amiss, but it didn't feel like I'd gone to another world. This world had pink-haired and white-antlered Miriam's signature all over. Flowers I've never seen dotted the landscape. The sky wasn't quite the blue of any natural sky. Clouds seemed an afterthought. The trees were either in springtime bloom or twisted, strange things. One spread its branches and started walking away. What I at first thought were fireflies, were little winged people. Sprites.

"Olympus is just as bizarre to an Earth dweller," Miriam said. "I was in awe the first time I went. This is another universe like the one occupied by Olympus, Hades, and Atlantis."

I shook my head in disbelief, asking the obvious, "Atlantis is real?"

"It is where Poseidon reigns," Lucinda confirmed. She waved to the handsome fae prince, who was lying in the meadow next to the young woman with curly, dyed hair and the old-soul eyes.

Another young woman with close-cropped blue hair sat with them, watching their interaction. All the youthful angst in that one. She wanted a future with a happy, settled family—lots of kids. The poor thing wouldn't get one if she kept company with the other girl. Power radiated from her. She was a demigod. All my grandmother's stories taught me, gods and demigods didn't stay with mortals long. They preferred their kind. The fae seemed like a father to the girls, but their appearances and whatever they were besides human told otherwise.

Hovering protectively close to the trio, a stern looking man of striking features and action movie body stared in my direction with his arms crossed over a bare, muscly chest.

I recognized him. He was one of the nephilim and a wolf shifter —though I hadn't seen him in wolf form—the Archangel of the Americas, Gabriel Crowfoot. That meant the girls were Roxanne Crowfoot and Jada Diaz, junior council members and the daughters of Gabriel and Miriam. I started putting names to all the supes around me, Aurora was the bigfoot. Leilani, the Hawaiian demigoddess, and Cian, a leprechaun, were a married couple on the council. Shawn and Micah were also married and some sort of auxiliary members of the council.

A shudder ran through me.

This council were as close to a governing body for supernaturals as any mundane government were to schmoes like me. According to the news, they worked with the International Supernatural Enforcement Agency—the cops for the supe world. I might as well be facing the president of the United States. These were the last people a former fake fortune teller, who didn't know how to work her oracle gift, wanted to be around.

Phyr approached. "Yeah?"

"Lydia left her belonging in that car we saw. Think you can fetch them for her before we take her back?" Lucinda asked.

"They're all I own," I added, unsure if he cared. He'd seemed kind, but people aren't always what they seem.

The fae prince regarded me for a moment with intense amber eyes before nodding. He karate chopped the air and then disappeared. Within moments, he reappeared with my bags and purse.

Miriam gasped behind me then walked up to the bag with my grandparents' memorabilia.

I clenched my hands into fists. "Don't touch that. It's priceless."

She turned to me, glowing green eyes scrutinizing. "What kind of magic is imbued in the objects within?"

"I've never seen that color either," Phyr added.

Gabriel moved closer, his gaze sweeping between my stuff, Miriam, Phyr, and me. Suddenly everyone focused on me and my bag of nostalgia.

"My grandparents brought the things from their village in Greece. I don't know about magic, but they were passed down to me and all I have left of my family. Please, if they have magic, I don't know how to wield it."

Gabriel called for the council members to confer outside my hearing range.

Phyr stayed with me. I doubt it was to keep me company.

I wrung my hands. A fierce, mean part of me said to take my belongings and zap them. I shoved that part down. I didn't want any more trouble, especially from monsters.

"When an object is imbued with strange magic, it makes people nervous. When you have a whole suitcase filled with them and don't know what spellwork was cast, it must be discussed."

"I'm telling the truth."

"I know." He tapped his head.

"Are you some sort of lie detector, " I quipped.

A corner of his mouth ticked up. Mischief glittered in his amber eyes. "I'm used to supernaturals knowing about my kind. First time speaking to a fae?"

I narrowed my eyes, scrutinizing Phyr. Never had I ever been so open and honest with anyone. It was like I was some sort of green-horn, who hadn't lived around wise guys for the past twenty years.

"You can read thoughts, can't you?"

He inclined his head. "I can ease your worries, too. I'm not allowed to practice my gifts on mundanes, but supes of your heritage get no reprieve. The Olympians you serve should teach you how to block others out. You're defenseless with your mind open like that."

I crossed my arms over my chest and shrank within myself, suddenly not liking Phyr at all. I imagined my skull made of impenetrable armor, blocking him and anyone else out.

He clapped his hands. "There you go, Lydia! My, you're a quick learner and look at that defense. So skilled."

A smile touched my own lips. I couldn't help it. He'd let me know a weakness when he could've kept exploiting it. Perhaps I was right to trust him, but only a little.

His head snapped to the right. Miriam's head snapped in the same direction. Then we all heard rolling thunder. A fiery blur shot past, faster than my eyes could track.

Phyr drew a sword. Green light shimmered down the length of his blade. The fae's eyes shifted from amber to radiating the same green light. His casual clothes slipped away, revealing leather armor with fancy green scrawl lit up like L.E.D strips in a cosplay.

Hermes suddenly stood among the fray gathered around my luggage. Bright magenta light glowed where his eyeballs had been and his voice amplified as if he were talking through a megaphone when he demanded, "Where is the Oracle?"

The Supernatural Council of the Americas all pointed in my direction.

In a blink he stood in front of me, assessing me for—injuries?
"What?"

Suddenly, he was in my space. The god really had to stop buzzing around so fast. I was about to tell him so when I saw genuine worry etched on his face.

"Are you harmed?"

The concern made me grin. I couldn't help it. I liked that he worried about me enough to come looking. "A little worse for wear, but I'm good. How did you know where to find me?"

"I always know where you are...If I look." Before I could ask what he meant by that, Hermes turned his back to me to face the council. "Why was the Oracle detained against her will in this realm?"

"We rescued the Oracle from the clutches of Echidna and Typhon, Herald of Olympus" Lucinda replied, tilting her chin upward.

"Echidna and Typhon are in Tartarus, siren," he spat, his anger a palpable thing. "If this is a plot of your queen, she should be aware Zeus himself has taken interest in this one and has assigned me her protector. We tire of our oracles dying."

I shuddered. From my grandmother's stories of his exploits, Zeus didn't sound like a god that I wanted taking interest in me.

Lucinda rubbed her brow as if she were dealing with an irritating man rather than an angry god. "Oracles dying has nothing to do with my queen or her king. I saved the Oracle's life. Ask her."

I stammered for a second, not prepared to speak quite yet. "It's true. Jen-monster and Snake-man kidnapped me. These guys fought the monsters then and took me here."

"Describe these so-called monsters," Hermes asked in a gentler tone than he'd used with the others.

"I uh—" Instead of giving him a description, I told him what happened from the snakes in my motel room, to my kidnapping, and finally to the rescue.

Hermes listened, frowning.

He turned to Lucinda. "She should have been brought to Olympus or at least to your queen. Again, why did you bring the Oracle to a faerie where she is helpless to their kind?"

Lucinda's resolve wavered a little. Wavered, the way someone who had divided loyalties would if they showed favor to one side over the other and got called on it.

"The kidnapping happened on our world," Gabriel replied, speaking for the first time, "Olympus and Hades have a treaty with the Supernatural Council of the Americas. The treaty stipulates that any crimes committed in our territory will be investigated by this council. This was the safest place to bring her."

Hermes was undeterred. "I know the treaty. You were to notify us if an Olympian or one of ours is involved in the crime "

"I would have sent a dove as soon as we were done with our investigation," Lucinda replied.

"But, you came into my faerie without invitation," Miriam added, something old and powerful creeping into her voice. Her features shifted ever so slightly. "Without provocation."

The hairs on the back of my neck stood up. I didn't have to be able to read the future to know this could go sideways fast.

"I came for the Oracle," Hermes protested, gesturing to me. "As Lydia's protector, I have every right to seek her and see to her safety wherever she may be."

My protector? I almost rolled my eyes. So much for me having to protect myself and letting the journey teach me.

Gabriel sidled next to Miriam, a little protective in his own stance. "Olympus failed to notify the council of the identity of the new Oracle."

Hermes spread his arms. "Do you blame us with our most recent oracle murdered in your domain?"

I didn't understand politics, but I understood the question was an accusation and that this situation was bigger than me. This much fuss wasn't just over my safety. The office I so blithely signed up for seemed much too important for me to disappear. My stomach knotted. There wouldn't be a loophole to get out of this contract, but I could fix the argument happening here.

"Those monsters knew I was the Oracle. They called me the key. I think they killed my mom." I should have included the key bit before, but I rushed through my explanation.

Everyone quieted.

"Where are the Titans now?" Hermes asked.

"Detained in a prison of my making," Miriam replied.

The god trembled. "They escaped *Tartarus*. You think a realm of an infant's making could hold not one, but *two* Titans?"

The Supernatural Council of the Americas all exchanged glances.

For some reason they must have believed Miriam's power was absolute because judging by their expressions, they had not thought about where the titans had escaped from. Miriam and Phyr exchanged a look. Phyr swiped a hand in the air, disappearing and reappearing shortly after. All humor I'd seen in his handsome bronze face vanished with his return.

"They're gone."

Lucinda's jaw went slack. The others appeared just as shocked.

Hermes shook his head, radiating disapproval. "In your hubris, you have let two primordial beings with no regard for mortal lives loose on all the realms. Worse, they will stop at nothing to open the gates to Tartarus. We will see the end to all that we know. I must warn Olympus."

My heart sank. I thought he'd leave me again. Instead, Hermes gathered and lifted my belongings.

Everyone forgot about the contents of my suitcases, or at least, let their curiosity go. Titans were loose. They had to prepare.

That left me no choice but to go with the god to Olympus.

"Hold me," Hermes said in Greek, his tone gentle.

I wrapped my arms around his neck, aware of every inch of the god that pressed against me. His gaze locked with mine for several breaths, I thought he was going to kiss me.

Instead, he lifted me and ran.

THIRTEEN

I almost threw up on Hermes' hard-muscled pecs. I couldn't help it. My brain was not meant to process the roads he traveled to get to Olympus. I used the word "road" loosely. It was dark, cold, and the only air was what Hermes exhaled into my face.

Yet, I felt safe the whole time. The safest I'd felt since the last time I was in his arms.

No. No. That would *not* do.

He may have made lots of claims about my protection, but I didn't know him. His interest in me began and ended in my position of oracle—a tenuous thing since I couldn't control my gift.

As soon as he stopped moving, I disentangled myself from Hermes, turning to take in my surroundings.

We ended up in a gleaming, white marble room. Potted plants hung from golden chains. A single blue chaise was the only furniture, but the walls had shelves with vases, statues, and painted discs much like one would see in a museum. The air smelled fresh and crisp. Water gurgled somewhere beyond the walls and harp music drifted in.

"This is the antechamber to my quarters," Hermes explained. "I thought you could wait here while I speak to The Twelve."

The twelve chairs of the Olympus throne. Hermes was one of them.

"Sure! I love being in strange places alone." I wasn't being sarcastic. My enthusiasm to do anything but speak to the gods poured from every syllable.

An amused smile touched his lips. His eyes were his eyes again, brown irises and white sclerae. The corners crinkled. "You're strange."

I quirked an eyebrow. "Have you seen you when your eyes get all glowy and your voice thundery?"

He blinked, cocking his head. "What?"

I snort-laughed. "You were all Herald to the Gods back there."

He licked his lips. Somehow, he seemed closer without moving. His voice changed. "Impressed with my godly might, were you?"

Warmth radiated from my insides and thoughts I hadn't thought in years surfaced. *No. No. No. Lydia!*

I'd just gotten out of a bad marriage. Besides, Hermes was a *god*, and I was only a—well, the Olympians didn't exactly have a good track record of sticking it out.

"Are you flirting with me?"

His eyes darkened with something I hadn't experienced from a man in a long time. Desire. His voice a velvet purr, when he asked, "Would you like me to flirt with you?"

My gaze swept over his body. I couldn't help it. He was a freaking literal Greek god, and he was *flirting* with me. So what if the ink hadn't dried on my divorce papers yet? I'm only human.

I swallowed hard and nodded. "Oh, yes I do."

A part of me felt promiscuous. I told that part to take a hike. Carlo gave back the ring and that side of our marriage ended years ago. A god. A literal god had the hots for me. Rebound or bad idea, I didn't care. I was *not* turning Hermes down.

I yipped as he swept me in his arms. The movement so fast, my brain hadn't processed it.

"Can I kiss you?"

I nodded.

His lips pressed into mine; soft, sweet, and swiftly over, leaving me wanting more.

Hermes drew back, his dark eyes searching mine.

I panted, breathless from a peck. Not pathetic at all.

His playful expression hardened to that of a serious, imposing god. "Flirtation implies an affair, hot and bright. Such loves burn out as quickly as they ignite—leaving regret and heartbreak in the ashes."

He took a heaving breath and I swear to everything holy my knees turned to jelly with that sigh.

Hermes continued, "I am fast in the way I get from place to place, but I am not quick to love and not easy to tire of my lovers. Although I find promise of all I yearn for in your lips." He caressed my cheek with a tender hand. "I cannot indulge in a fleeting romance with you. I'll want more. I know it."

Hermes didn't give me a chance to react, to even process what he said, before he zipped out of the antechamber.

Alone with my tumbling thoughts and whirlwind of emotions, I sat on the blue chaise. In the last three days, I'd been contacted by a Titan, almost got arrested, started having visions I couldn't control, kidnapped by monsters, rescued by monsters, and kissed by a smoking hot god, who spoke like a poet and didn't want a flash in the pan romance.

Antsy, I rose.

Hermes didn't say I couldn't explore. I found a massive golden door which led to a bedroom bigger than my entire apartment above the store in my old building. Opulent decor filled the room. Four posters with Greco-Roman style columns stood at the corners of an Olympic-sized bed. The bedding looked like real silk.

I rubbed the material between my fingers, groaning. It would be heavenly to sleep naked in a bed like this. Not that I'd slept naked in a long time.

I followed the open doors into a bathroom. "Pretty Woman!" I squealed. The tub looked as big as the one from the movie that Julia Roberts had bathed in. "What I wouldn't give to have a long soak right now!"

"Sorry, I can't fulfill your request. I don't speak that tongue," a dulcet voice said in modern Greek but strangely accented. The accent was reminiscent of the way Jen spoke her dialect of Greek.

A woman with blue-hued skin slipped from behind vines growing along the wall on my left. Her hair was almost the same color as the vines. Seashells covered her perky breasts and a pale skirt wrapped around shapely hips. Her eyes weren't the same green as her hair, but instead were the color of lily pads. Thin lines marked her neck. Upon her approach, I realized the markings were moving gills.

"It wasn't a request. I was wishing out loud," I replied in Greek, smiling. The gills unnerved me, but I probably seemed strange to her too. The poor thing was probably an Olympian housekeeper. "I don't need anything. I'm just waiting for Hermes. Have a nice day."

The stranger's eyes lit up and she clapped her hands enthusiastically as if I'd performed a trick. "You speak the tongue of the gods prettily, Oracle." She practically pounced on me, embracing me in a bear hug. For a tiny thing, she was exceptionally strong. "You're so kind to wish me a good day. I love you!"

"Um, thank you?" I patted her back. Something told me she didn't get out of Olympus, or perhaps this bathroom, much.

The hug for no reason reminded me of my kiddo, Luke. I missed my boy fiercely in that moment. Missed any sense of normalcy.

She drew back. "Apologies." Horror twisted her features. A tear slid down her cheek. "I touched the Ichor without permission."

I waved off her concern. "No worries. Nothing wrong with being affectionate."

"Nymphs cannot touch The Ichor. The queen wouldn't like it," the woman whispered, batting large, wet eyes.

"What I don't like," an imperious voice echoed through the washroom. The sound of shoes clicked on the marble. "Are nymphs slipping into the bed of the king, trying to curry favor to become what they are not."

The blue nymph squeaked, gills flaring along with her eyes. She scurried off, disappearing behind the vines.

I twirled to see that an obscenely tall woman with the body of an athlete had entered the bathroom. A golden laurel circlet topped a head of loose, dark curls. Her features and demeanor seemed matronly more than regal. Her face and smile were as warm and tender as a mother's love. Her chiton was lovely shade of lavender and she smelled of fresh flowers as she approached.

I held absolutely still, not daring to even breathe. There was one queen in Olympia and her name was Hera. My grandmother taught me all of Hera's blessings: marriage, motherhood, all that of hearth and home. She also taught me of Hera's wrath, her jealousy, and her harsh punishments of Zeus's lovers. The goddess wasn't someone I wanted to piss off. The sooner I could be out of her sight, and the fewer chances of me doing something wrong, the better.

"That nymph would gain your trust, become your best friend, and then turn around and tell Zeus all your weaknesses, hopes, and insecurities. My husband would then use that knowledge to seduce you. Not because he has any desire for your flesh. Our king's amorous days are long over. He's promised so. Again." A bitter laugh escaped her lips, at odds with her kindly face. It gave her wholesome features the air of a mask about to crack.

"However, Zeus does love the power an oracle can give him— humans do so love to know the measure of their mortal strand and their belief—" She paused, casting midnight eyes in the direction of a window. Outside, the nymph had joined others like herself in a stream. "No others can match human belief. Zeus wants their adoration and fear again. Be wary, Oracle. My husband's game is old, and he makes the same tired plays, but he always wins."

I nodded slowly, not daring to speak.

Hera turned on her heel, pausing at the door. Over her shoulder, she tossed, "Don't let anyone here know about the treasures in your care. They left Olympia for a reason. See that they don't return."

At this, I found my voice. "Why are you warning me?"

Hera looked ahead, so I couldn't see her face. "No one ever warned me."

FOURTEEN

After Hera left, I scurried into the antechamber, grabbing my belongings and hauling them into Hermes' bedroom. The doors to the room had no locks. I shut them anyways. I drew the drapes to the window. Bone weary, I sank onto the bed. My whole body developed new ways to whine, my muscles and joints displeased with the last—seventy? —hours. Flopping on my back dramatically, my exhale rushed from my lungs in a loud whoosh.

"I'm too old for this shit."

Dione had said something about how Hera was not to be trusted, but Hera didn't ask anything of me. She'd only warned me. I'd read people long enough to know she'd risked something with that warning. What though? Everyone knew Zeus was a horn dog. The ancient Greeks loved writing about his gross exploits. Did women still get seduced by him, when he had such an infamous track record?

Maybe the very dumb or young or both.

I closed my eyes.

When I opened them again, my face was smashed against a pillow. My mouth tasted like hot garbage. Sitting up, I smacked my lips and then wiped my hand across my mouth to wipe away the drool. A noticeable stain darkened the pillowcase. Well, that ought to disabuse Hermes of any notion of burning passions for me.

I snickered at my own joke.

"Amusing dream or do you find waking in my brother's bed hilarious?" someone drawled. "You should be honored. Hermes rarely allows anyone in here."

The stranger lounging in a chair in the corner of the room had the appearance of a Greco-Roman statue brought to life. Thankfully, he wore a belted peplos, so I didn't have to see his bits.

I was getting really tired of running into supernaturals who were grossly more attractive than I was, and more importantly had the upper hand. I had always liked living in my poor little corner of whatever town I landed in, because I knew the deal. This was a whole new game, one where I didn't know the rules and had only heard of the players.

Eyeing the lyre the stranger strummed casually, I said, "I was enjoying a little self-deprecating humor, Apollo."

He flashed straight white teeth that gleamed. His face grew exponentially more handsome with that smile. "Given the number of my siblings who play the lyre, excellent guess."

I bowed with a flourish. "Excuse me, I must, er, take care of necessities."

"I'll wait here." Apollo nodded and returned to strumming his lyre. The song was heartachingly beautiful and perfect in every way. Of course. He was the god of the arts.

Cool. Awesome. I was hanging out with a god in another god's bedroom. Tooooootally normal.

I found a small water closet with a toilet within the grand bathing room. Thank goodness gods went pee. My bladder would have forced me to find the nearest vase, which wouldn't be the politest, let alone the sexiest, thing to do to someone I'm interested in. After taking care of necessities, washing up, taming my hair as best as possible, and brushing my teeth with some sweet-smelling twigs, I returned to Hermes' bedroom.

True to his word, Apollo still strummed his lyre where I'd left him. Why couldn't he be like most men and taken a hike.

"The oracles used to be mine," he said, hazel eyes meeting my gaze. "Hermes stole them like he steals everything else."

I didn't know how to reply, so I said what I'd say whenever Luke said something strange as a kid. "Interesting."

"Indeed. We had a lovely time. The bond between the Oracles of Delphi went beyond friendship. I loved a few very much. Sired and raised children with them. I loved some of those children enough to gift them objects of great power."

I stiffened, forcing my eyes to not go to the suitcases. In my periphery, the luggage remained where I left it. Did gods have the same x-ray superpowers as the fae?

"Every parent's wish is to keep their children safe." I knew I wanted to keep Luke safe, so much so I let him go when he went to college. Carlo and I had the kind of lifestyle where we could have followed our son, but neither Luke nor Carlo would have wanted that.

The corners of Apollo's shapely mouth turned down slightly. "A human sentiment. Most Titans did not possess such feelings for their offspring. Kronos ate his." He strummed a haunting melody on the lyre.

"Self-fulfilling prophecy. If Kronos hadn't eaten his children, maybe Zeus wouldn't have overthrown him."

Apollo shot me a reproachful glare. "*Tsk tsk.* Prophecies are what keep oracles relevant. I hope you've learned to hone your gift. It'll be useless if you can't control what thread you read from the weave."

I swallowed hard. He'd said relevant, but I understood he meant alive.

The god stood, setting the lyre on the chair. "Stop looking like I'm going to eat you." His gaze flicked to my suitcase, but only briefly. "You are precious to me, daughter."

I coughed, choking on my own disbelief. "Sorry. What did you just call me?"

He chuckled, the sound as musical and rich as the lyre. "Well, I can't say a thousand times great granddaughter. That would sound ridiculous."

"I'm related to Hermes?" I hadn't meant to say it out loud, but that made the best kiss of my life kinda gross.

"As related as you are related to all humanity. It's too distant to count." His eyes swept over me. Regret limned his features. For what, I didn't know, until he opened his big trap and said, "With my blood running through your veins, you must have been a great beauty...in your youth."

I opened my mouth to shoot a sarcastic reply, thought better of it, and shut it before I got myself in trouble.

Apollo offered a muscular yet supple arm. "Come dear, it's time for you to meet those you serve."

The palace of the Olympians sprawled a seemingly endless expanse. In the marble halls, we passed nymphs of various hues of the rainbow. I tried not to stare at their extraordinary, inhuman features, but the nymphs and my surroundings were marvelous to behold. The architecture varied from classical Greek to whimsical and nonsensical.

Fountains flowed upward and sideways. A myriad of butterflies flitted down one corridor, or what I'd assumed were butterflies. Much like the fireflies of Miriam's faerie, the insects of Olympus were not always what they seemed.

With so many inhabitants to rule over in the palace alone, why did the gods care about Earth and a prediction of an oracle from that world? Why give her immortality? Usually, I could figure out a person or a group's angle. The oracle business wasn't adding up. Was I a fall guy of some sort? That thought troubled me.

What troubled me more was that the Titans didn't harm me or even threaten me. Jen—er—Echidna called me "the key" and told me I was "safe". When trouble came in the form of the Supernatural Council of the Americas, Echidna hid me and put a wall of snakes between me and whatever.

However, what were the two Titans going to do with me at the mouth of Tartarus? Did they want me to free the rest of their kind? How could I, a person with no superpowers up until this point, and still not able to use them at will, achieve anything but embarrassment?

My stomach knotted the same way it did whenever I had a feeling Carlo's latest scheme wouldn't work. My premonitions about which cons would work and which ones wouldn't, weren't always accurate. Having that tight ball in the pit of my stomach now didn't bode well.

I had to stop letting these gods push me around, I had to figure out their angles and fast. I wasn't a powerful being like them, but I was smart and would need to use those smarts to outwit whatever machinations were going on around me, or face the same fate that befell my mother.

CHAPTER

FIFTEEN

Gods and their kin packed the throne room of the palace. I was in Olympus. Vertigo set in. Surreal didn't cover how I felt. There were no words. Never would I imagine that I would be walking among the characters of the bedtime stories of my youth any more than I thought I would walk down the aisle of the Academy Awards, rubbing elbows with celebrities.

Some turned and stared, others carried on their conversations, but many casually glanced in my direction. The band around my stomach cinched tighter. No sane person would want this much attention from so many powerful entities.

Maybe Carlo. If my erstwhile husband believed he could work an angle, he would. He'd also get so caught up in getting the score, he would forget who he was dealing with and get burnt. No wonder he got caught.

Anger, hot and bright, flared in my chest. If Carlo hadn't put me in such a precarious position, I wouldn't have signed the contract. I could've taken the bus to Seattle and moved in with Luke and Juan by now. Some of that rage pointed inward. If I had remembered the moral of at least one tale my grandparents had told me, I would have remembered there are no loopholes—not without a dire price.

I lifted my chin. No. I've never allowed my life to become a tragedy before. I was a survivor, over forty years old and eking a living for almost thirty. This contract wouldn't end me. I just needed the power players' angles to develop my own.

Scanning the gathered crowd, I delved into deep memories, recalling who was who and observing how they reacted to me. Sometimes the not-so-top-brass players could provide excellent allies and information gatherers. Everyone who didn't sit on the twelve thrones on the dais all wanted to be there, whether they admitted it or not. They wouldn't be in this room otherwise.

Apollo brought me onto the dais where none stepped foot except, he, Hermes, and I. The three of us stood several steps below another platform where twelve thrones faced the entire room.

At the center, a gray bearded god eyed me. Zeus was impossibly handsome yet had a fatherly air about him. He oozed sexuality. All Zeus needed was a leather jacket, jeans, some tattoos, and a misogynistic t-shirt to be a hog-riding Daddy. A strange look for a god.

He was also an older version of the god all the priestesses lined up to mount in my dream. It didn't feel like a dream now. I could almost smell him then and now.

On Zeus's left, Hera watched me with interest. Her demeanor suggested she'd never seen me before. Okay. The Queen of the gods wanted our little tête-à-tête kept secret.

I'd oblige.

For now.

Apollo climbed the stairs, taking a throne to the right of Zeus. Another empty throne must belong to Hermes, who stayed on the same dais as I stood.

A dark-haired goddess in a chiton, with a bow and quiver next to her throne, watched Apollo through slitted eyes. Artemis was the goddess of the hunt. She paid me little attention.

Good. I didn't feel like being hunted.

Next to her, a goddess with ash blonde hair and dressed in full armor, watched me like a full cat watches a mouse. Not ready to strike, but mindful of where her next meal went. That would be wise Athena.

Next to Athena sat two more goddesses, I figured were Demeter and Hestia. On Hera's left sat a large warrior. Ares. A voluptuous goddess with pouty lips and doe eyes next to him, one whom I guessed was Aphrodite, sat between the warrior Ares and the blacksmith Hephaestus. Awkward. If the stories were true, Zeus made Aphrodite marry Hephaestus, but she had a continual love affair with Ares, not to mention countless others.

Ares's attention laid on the rise and fall of Aphrodite's chest. By the look in his eyes, I highly doubted he was concerned about her respiration rate.

Aphrodite's gaze passed between me and Hermes. A smile touched her lips as her eyes met mine. She winked. I didn't know why or what the goddess of love wanted, but it was plain that the wink made Hermes uncomfortable.

He sidled a step closer to me.

Next to Aphrodite, Hephaestus propped his head on his fist, his gaze distant.

Carlo would get that way sometimes when we'd take Lukie on outings or at school functions. His mind was always somewhere else, plotting and scheming. I stopped inviting my then-husband on outings. Not forcing Carlo to be an involved dad was easier on us all.

The two outermost thrones, marked with a trident on one and a cloak on the other, remained empty. Although Hades and Poseidon ruled other realms, Zeus kept a place of highest importance for his brothers on Olympus.

A different water nymph than the one in Hermes room brought a covered platter onto the dais where Hermes and I stood. The god of crossroads and herald to Olympus scowled at the bowl.

"Is this necessary father?"

"Oracles are liars," Athena answered with no venom in the statement. She made the gross generalization with as little emotion as you'd say the lines are long at Target, a known, annoying fact, but not anything to be upset about.

The statement stung. One, because Athena had been one of my favorite goddesses. Two, because I had been a liar for a living.

"Will you vouch this one has lived an honorable life worthy of our trust?" Zeus asked, voice rumbling.

Hermes put himself physically between me and the bowl. "This will tell us what will happen not what has happened."

Zeus rubbed his brow. I did this when Luke would bring up ridiculous arguments in his teen years. The king of the gods exhaled a long-suffering sigh. "It's not that I don't believe your story. The past cannot be changed but what happens next can. Take your place, Herald."

Hermes hesitated. I could feel his objection forming.

Soft murmurs broke out in the crowd

"Oh, brother. Don't reveal your heart so openly," Apollo said in a bored tone. "Father won't hurt your pet. Let her do her job."

I touched his back. "It's okay."

It wasn't but I didn't want Hermes getting in trouble over something I'd signed myself over to do.

Hermes shot me a sympathetic glance before taking his seat among the ruling gods.

Another nymph placed a tripod seat behind me. "Sit, please."

I did, only because I had no other choice.

Zeus rose from his chair and descended the stairs. He regarded me fondly. "I mean you no harm, my precious child."

His dark eyes, kindly and paternal, the warmth in them reminding me of my grandfather. Up close, I swore I saw similarities. I mentally shook my head and reinforced the barriers that Phyr had taught me to place.

The king's smile dropped, almost imperceptibly. I doubt an average human would catch it. Thirty years of telling fortunes taught me to pick up even the slightest shift in a person's face.

"I believe you, but I'll bet there are a few in here that aren't ready to be best buds with me."

Zeus laughed, a hearty sound. His mirth didn't reach his eyes. Suspicion lingered there.

Wow. This god was faking for the rest. Interesting. When I was a child, I imagined Zeus doing whatever he wanted, because he was the most powerful god. That's what king meant to me then. I had no idea that the person running things always had to watch their back. It took watching Carlo and his crew to learn that. Why should the gods be any different? Which meant Zeus was as shrewd as he was fake. You didn't become the King of the Gods and stay there, if you weren't sharper than the average.

I met his suspicion unflinchingly. I may not know how to use my powers, but they needed me to know what their enemies were planning. I just hoped I wouldn't give too much of myself away when I went into Prophecy Mode.

The suspicion turned to a curious tilt of his head. Smiling, Zeus offered me his hand. "Read the weave for me, Oracle."

Tentatively, I laid mine in his. I expected some sort of electric shock or surge of power to emanate from the mighty Zeus. His skin felt warm and soft, but no different from the skin of any human I'd ever touched. No extra power vibes.

Were humans formed by the gods in their image, or were gods formed by ours?

Zeus shot the nymph an impatient look. The fawn-colored woman scurried closer, lifting the lid from the bowl.

The noxious odor of sulfur hit my nostrils. My eyes teared with the strength of the stench. My vision blurred, colors swirling into a gray mass. I fought against the soporific tide rolling over me. I wanted to be conscious for this, to experience the visionary prophecy, more importantly to know what I told the gods. One human cannot fight the will of the gods. The darkness pulled me under.

CHAPTER
SIXTEEN

The valley had once been peaceful. A meadow between Mount Olympus and Mount Othrys. The azure sky darkened to the color of muddied water. Thunder clapped and streaks of lightning announced the Olympian's approach.

Zeus with this thunderbolt, Poseidon with his trident, and Adonieus with his bident.

We answered in kind, showing our might. Still a tremor of fear shuddered through me. Why did each generation have to usurp the former and destroy that which forged them?

Over a prophecy.

Always a prophecy.

They had imprisoned their own parents—our parents.

What mercy would they show us?

From high on Othrys, I watched my beautiful siblings throw themself into battle with the three brothers and the goddesses. I remained unmoving, unwilling to fight against him.

Loving Zeus had been my greatest mistake and most treasured experience. He was of the new and I was of the old, but we had tried to make a life together and created children together. I couldn't move against *him. Even now, with Hera at his side. the one he chose over me, fighting against my family. I loved Zeus too much and that would be my downfall.*

I turned from the battle. Running from the fight betrayed my siblings down there risking everything to keep our freedom, but I was a mother. My children's safety came before my duty and loyalty to anyone else. I fled, running without looking back. I prayed to our lost parents that my siblings would win.

In my secret heart, I knew they wouldn't, yet I was glad. Zeus wouldn't ever imprison me. He may be my weakness, but I was his too.

Two Olympians headed toward the cave where I'd hid my offspring.

"MY CHILDREN!" I startled to my feet, smacking my head on something hard.

"It's alright. We're going to your kid." A hand pulled at me.

I rubbed my aching head with my free hand and took in my surroundings. I headbutted an overhead storage compartment.

"Please put your seat in the upright position and fasten your seatbelts. It's a clear and sunny day in Denver. We'll be taking off in..."

No. No. No. I hated flying.

Passengers all stared at me, doe eyed.

The blue-nymph from the throne room held my hand from her aisle seat. Except she didn't look like a nymph anymore. She had somehow morphed into an olive-skinned human with large brown eyes and traded in her chiton for a pink tracksuit—not to mention, a bad bleach job.

Tired of gods and monsters dragging me this way and that, I ripped my hand from hers. "You can't fool me, nymph." I tapped my head. "I remember."

She smiled in that condescending way people do when they think you're stupid, yet her eyes darted around nervously. In the cautious tone you use with toddlers and psychopaths, she said, "Francine, I'm your sister, Rhonda."

"Like hell you are." Remembering what Hera said about my grandparents' memorabilia, I hastily scanned my surroundings. There! In the overhead compartment across the aisle, I spotted my luggage.

A leg stuck out, blocking my path. Rhonda held her hands up. "I'm your sister. We're on an airplane. You're on medication that's confusing you. Sit down and I'll explain."

"I did what I was supposed to do. There's no reason to be going anywhere with you."

Her perfect smile faltered. "We're taking you home to Seattle, remember?"

A flight attendant in his mid-twenties leaned over, smiling way too wide. "Ma'am. We're going to require you to take a seat and buckle-up. Captain's orders."

I shook my head. "I'm not supposed to be here."

The nymph grabbed my hand and spritzed something in my face. My vision blurred. Vertigo set in. My legs collapsed. I was vaguely aware of hitting the seat as I got sucked under once again.

I CAME to consciousness more slowly this time, finding myself in a small, yellow room that smelled of antiseptic. My heart leapt in my chest. I broke out in a cold sweat. Where was I now? I noticed my luggage propped on either side of an uncomfortable metal chair. I sat up and looked out the window of a door to my left. Judging by their uniforms, two TSA officers chatted with the nymph-who-now-looked-human just outside. I realized I was in a detainment room for airport security. Great. All they had to do was run my ID and find out that I was wanted in connection to Carlo's scheme.

"I told you my sister is unwell. She's on medication that causes disorientation and confusion, sleep talking. She isn't violent. I'm not violent. We pose no threat to ourselves or others." She waved papers in one hand and what looked like two passports in another. Likely false documents, proving I was under her care and whatever ID she had made up for her story.

The officers nodded along, but I could read in their faces that they were humoring her. She was going to be under arrest as soon as she gave them enough to book her.

I had to get out of there.

Something occurred to me. I grinned. They hadn't read me my Miranda rights or told me I was under arrest. The fawn obviously had a fake identity for me. All I had to do was leave and they'd never know who escaped.

Head still spinning, I rose on wobbly legs.

Conveniently, there was a door behind me with "exit" overhead. Shouldering my purse and grabbing my luggage, I tiptoed to the door.

The door opened into an airport filled with milling people. A cacophony of fly-by conversations, overhead announcements, small vehicles carting the disabled, music from a store all hit me at once. Taking no time to adjust, I ducked into the flow of human traffic going toward another exit sign, leading to escalators. The escalator dumped us onto a subway train terminal.

I chewed my lip, unsure if I wanted to get on. From the signage I gleaned I was back in Denver, which didn't make me feel too good about my mental state. All that had transpired since I left Denver, just to end up back there. It almost felt like a delusion.

I shook my head internally. No. That woman didn't look like a nymph, but she wasn't my sister either. My mother didn't have any more children, or Dione wouldn't have come to me

There were another set of escalators going up. I considered going back up and finding another exit. Following the crowd was the only way that I wouldn't be easily detected by security cameras. Right then, I appeared like anyone else. Taking the escalator up, while the general crowd waited, would get noticed.

While I stared at the escalators, debating what to do next, I spied the two TSA officers who had been talking to the nymph on the level above. A chime rang and the doors behind me whooshed open. Decision made, I spun around, and filed inside the train with the erstwhile waiting crowd.

CHAPTER

SEVENTEEN

Cramped in the standing room only train, I held onto my suitcases rather than the pole provided. That's the nice thing about having broad hips and sturdy legs, they make for a good base for balance. As the doors opened at the first stop, my heart leapt in my chest. Expecting to see officers waiting to arrest me but finding none, I sighed with relief.

Most of the passengers unloaded, leaving me with room to sit. Before I took a seat, I debated disembarking. The map above the door indicated there were three more stops, the last outside the main building in Lot A. Lot A it was. I took a seat and stowed my bags between my legs, and I put my purse on my lap. No sooner than I got was situated, the train took off again.

I hoped I appeared casual on the outside because I was quaking on the inside—My nerves were on high alert at every stop.

At least my features were unremarkable. It was nice to have the same color hair and eyes as seventy-five percent of the people on the planet. Plus, women my age were grossly overlooked. Once gray threaded our hair and our middles thickened, we were deemed harmless and not as eye-catching as our youthful counterparts, which was fine by me. No more catcalls or attention from the authorities.

The next stop wasn't any easier. My heart drummed in my ears, and I exhaled only when the doors closed again. It was just me in the car at that point, but I couldn't relax. There were still two more stops until the fabled Lot A, but I was underground until then.

The lights flickered and then went out completely. Underground, I was in eerie darkness. Not even lights from the tunnel mitigated the pitch. The only grounding force was the noise and rocking of the train.

The train stopped rocking.

No comforting *click click* of the wheels on the rails.

My mouth went dry. Every hair on my body stood on end, and I broke out in a cold sweat. I hated total darkness almost as much as I hated complete silence. Ever since I'd moved in with my grandparents, I'd had a light in my room or fell asleep with the television on.

I felt for the handles of my bags and found them. In complete darkness, I stood without knowing where I'd go or what to do. On shaky legs, I headed in the direction in which I hoped would lead to the doors. I'd pry them open with my hands if I had to. There was no way I would get stuck on a subway let alone have the TSA arrest me while scared in the dark.

The doors released with a gasp. A purple light no bigger than a candle flame floated in, illuminating the car in an eerie glow.

I groaned despite my chattering teeth.

Another god or monster messing with me. *Great.*

The stench of sulfur that rolled in but preceded a more pleasant scent. The light grew. I could make out shapes heading to the door.

I never liked Halloween fun houses. It's not that I ever believed they were actually haunted. So much build up before the jump scare. It was the anticipation that got me.

While I was under the influence of the siren, I vaguely recalled zapping the snakes imprisoning me. I wish I knew how I did it. A lightning bolt would come in real handy right now. Anything would do. I wondered what power I had in my suitcases, why Hera thought my grandparents' stuff needed to be away from Olympus.

Low to the ground, three sets of glowing red eyes accompanied the sound of an animal panting and the distinct paw beat of a loping dog. A large one, judging by the ruckus.

Every instinct screamed to run, yet I was frozen in place as huge paws slammed into my chest. My arms flew up as I fell backward. Pain shot from the back of my skull, blinding me. My vision cleared but the headache from the impact didn't go away. Not to mention, I was pinned to the floor by a massive canine.

All three heads of the beast panted, revealing mouths of full of crazy sharp teeth and a lolling tongue. A globule of rancid drool hit my cheek.

"Gross!" I couldn't believe I'd managed to speak in my utter terror. Guess my revulsion toward bodily fluids out ick-factored my fear.

"Spot," a woman cried.

The creature made a noise that sounded more like "hurrum?" than a growl or bark. The question in the tone of the sound was so obvious that it felt I was under Scooby-Doo, not a three-headed monster about to devour me.

Then again, how many monsters were named Spot?

"I don't care how excited you are to meet her," a woman scolded in Greek—the stranger's voice raspy and deep. "It's poor manners to jump on her, and you know it!"

The erstwhile killer-canine's heads whimpered and stepped off me, not without licking my face with, not one, but all *three* disgusting tongues first.

The light shone in the car again, illuminating a woman about my height with black wavy hair that reached her waist. My goodness. I'd never dated a woman before, but this one made my heart race. Her face made the perfect oval. The symmetry of her features was flaw-less. Her light brown skin looked soft and her flesh supple. She had curves and beauty like I'd never seen, and I'd seen Aphrodite.

Midnight eyes gazed into mine as she offered me a hand.

I debated for about zero seconds and let the lovely stranger help me up. Our faces a breath a part, I couldn't help breathing in her scent. Oh gods, she smelled good, like lilies and rich spices.

Her dress was black and in the chiton style of the Olympians. Atop her shiny black hair, she wore a crown of Obsidian and black opal. Definitely a goddess. I wondered which one. The belt of her chiton was laurel and had leaves twined with pretty, white flowers. Were they the lilies I could smell?

Her mouth spread in a wide grin, setting little butterflies free in my stomach. "Cerberus likes you."

"He has a wonderful way of showing it." Reminded I had slobber all over my face, I wiped the drool with the back of my sleeve. Then it hit me who I was talking to. She was wearing a crown. She was wearing lilies or asphodel. Cerberus was the dog who guards Hades. There was only one queen of the underworld: Persephone. I added hastily, "Your majesty."

The artists throughout time liked to paint and sculpt Persephone as this doe-eyed innocent abducted by Hades. My grandparents had told a very different story of a young Olympian, who didn't want to be a fertility goddess and had tired of living in the shadow of her mother Demeter's Nature talents. So she seduced her uncle Adonieus, ruler of Hades, knowing Zeus wouldn't go against his brother. The goddess was simply Kore then, which meant "maiden". A generic and useless name of any temple woman. Now, as Persephone, her name meant "bringer of death", she ruled Hades with more severe punishments than her husband had ever. distributed.

The whole half of the year with her mother was bullshit, too, at least according to my grandparents. She got out of that bargain quickly, making all sorts of trouble for Hera and the gods until she got her way and could return to her husband. Come to think of it, my grandparents were the only ones who told the story like that.

I'd always admired Persephone. She saw a future she didn't like and struck out for the future she wanted.

Also, she would want the Oracle just as badly as her father.

"You know who I am then?"

It was posed as a question, but the goddess already knew my answer before I nodded in reply and said, "Persephone, Queen of Hades."

She flashed perfect teeth. "Then you know it's useless to do anything but agree when I ask you to come with me?"

I exhaled through my nose and nodded again.

Her erstwhile perfectly smooth brow wrinkled. It didn't diminish her beauty. "Unlike your time in Olympus, where I'm sure they have told you nothing, a conversation with me will prove beneficial to us both. I won't let any woman just bob along the water with no direction like an untethered boat. Come with me and you'll learn why the Olympians need you more than you need them."

CHAPTER
EIGHTEEN

Obsidian and glittering, Persephone's palace was the antithesis of the palace on Olympus. Wraiths in black cloaks, with hoods shielding their faces, floated in the lavish halls. Other specters acted as the living would, going about their business. Somehow, I wasn't afraid of any of the dead. Maybe because none of the inhabitants of the palace seemed unhappy. The conflict in Olympus seemed to not exist in Hades. The ruler of this domain, and the order of things, seemed clearer.

The halls were appointed with opulent décor throughout. They were a gothic dream with elements of nature throughout. Throughout her home, the Queen of Hades made life and death equally attractive. She brought me to a cozy room with comfy oversized chairs, offering one for me to sit. She took the other chair, sitting as much like a girlfriend ready to chat as a queen taking the throne. I liked not having to endure the pomp of Olympus despite the luxurious palace. I felt like I was in someone's home, not the chambers of a greater building.

Cerberus sat on the floor next to us. I noticed a patch of white in the shape of a diadem on his chest. His spot, earning the pooch his name. In my world, he only had one head. In the Underworld, he had three. Also, he'd grown a bit bigger and scarier, but only in appearance. Cerberus acted like a playful puppy, bringing me toys.

Lucky me.

"We live in uncertain times. Human belief is shifting. What was the norm for many millennia in your world is no longer so. There's a revival of the Greco-Roman gods, especially in the Americas where belief is, how do you say it, up for grabs." She smiled at her dog and scratched his ears. "My father once held great power. However, before the Olympians were the Titans. He fears humans worshipping those primordial gods." The smile faded. Her big brown eyes glistened, and her voice quavered as she added, "Since the only door to Tartarus is in my home, so do I."

I nodded, unsure of where this was going.

"I don't want a prediction, Lydia. I want to keep you safe from the Titans who escaped. If they use you as a key, you will die as certainly as your mother did." She exhaled a shaky breath. A tear fell. "Apollonia deserved better than whatever tortures Echidna and Typhon put her through trying to open the gate."

"How do you know she was tortured?"

Persephone rose and bid me to follow. We looked out a window. Below, in a beautiful twilight meadow dotted with asphodel, specters roamed. "Apollonia showed up at the Ferryman's Gate, her soul in tatters. She made little sense, a remnant more than a full soul, but she deserved peace."

I placed my palm on the window. The old wound in my chest ripped wide open and bleeding. Somewhere out there my mother wandered.

"Why do you care what happens to me or my mom?"

"The Oracles of Delphi possessed the ichor of the Fates, the Titans, the Olympians, and the blood of humans. The humans of the region, where your grandparents left, no longer have enough ichor for the sight. They long-ago lost faith in the gods of Olympus. You're the last oracle with enough of the ichor to see, and from what I hear, you can't control your power."

I kept a poker face, but inwardly I cringed. "What makes you say I can't control my power?"

"Fae can read minds and one shared with my general."

Well, Phyr, so much for trusting you.

"Don't worry. It's not a bad thing. You'll learn. It's not fair for you to be put in the middle of this fight when you have no choice. I know what that's like. I was forced to take the side of my husband or my mother. Their problems shouldn't have been mine, and neither should your ancestor's mistakes be yours, but here we both are."

My gaze returned to the fields below. Seems gods were not much different than humans. Persephone wanted us to relate, to make a connection. If I'd met the Queen of Hades first, I would have wanted that too. Her angle was to protect the underworld by protecting me since I'm "the key." I would have respected her more if she'd have admitted so instead of playing this friend angle. However, I did feel a modicum of gratitude that the queen kept my mother in asphodel, instead of the less desirable parts of Hades.

"When I return you to your world, Cerberus will join you. The Titans won't be able to abduct you so easily," She flashed straight white teeth in a not-quite smile. "Nor will any Olympians."

I reared my head. "Who on Olympus would it benefit to hurt me?"

A frown marred her pretty face. Her dark eyes regarded me with pity. "Not every Olympian adores my father. There are those who would see the Titans return just to make themselves the new hero. They tire of Zeus's reign and blame him for humans turning to the other gods. You were wise to leave that nymph behind."

I forced a halfhearted grin. Smart wasn't what I'd call any of this. I was used to controlling my life. Clients came to me. I got to assess them on my turf, and I was good at it. Even Carlo's shenanigans were predictable. This whole bouncing from place to place at the mercy of other people was getting old fast.

"About that. Can you take me to my mother's old place?"

"I cannot. I must return you to the time and place I found you. Your journey is important."

"Oh. Okay."

I didn't hide the disappointment that I felt. She could help me against Titans and Olympians, but the cops were *my* problem.

"What I can do is take you to your mother so that you may say goodbye and then return you to where I found you."

Her offer felt like sharp claws sinking into a festering wound. Even though I'd dreamed of what it would be like to meet my mother for years, I didn't know if I wanted to see Apollonia after she let me believe she was dead for forty years.

"You might learn something useful."

I nodded. I might. I might also learn that it hadn't hurt her at all to leave me and I didn't know if I could handle that.

DESPITE BEING FILLED WITH SHADES—BEINGS that are not quite ghosts and not quite solid entities anymore—the asphodel meadow was gorgeous. Set in an eternal sunset, everything had an amber hue to it. Fragrant flowers and bruised grass perfumed the air, as Persephone and I walked arm in arm through the fields.

We came upon a knoll with a cypress. A figure floated near the tree. My heart leapt at the sight of hair and a frame so similar to my grandmother's. I almost called to her. Almost. My grandmother was old when I was little. This woman, on the other hand, appeared younger than my current age. In fact, my mom looked a lot like she did in my hazy memories of her.

I furrowed my brow, turning to Persephone. "This shade is too young."

She nodded. "It's Apollonia. Oracles don't age after they take on their powers."

I rolled my eyes inwardly. Of course, I didn't become the Oracle when I had the youth and vigor—not to mention the lack of joint pain—of a nineteen-year-old. I would stay middle-aged forever.

My lighthearted resentment was brief, replaced by the shards of an old wound churning in my chest. The shade of my mother latched onto my gaze with hollow eyes.

CHAPTER
NINETEEN

Persephone wandered away discreetly, leaving me alone with the shade that was my mother. Unlike movie versions of ghosts, Apollonia was as substantial as me or anything else in our surroundings, or at least appeared so.

A part of me had the urge to rush to her and embrace her, to feel my mom's arms around me and know that sense of unconditional love I felt when she was alive. It's the child in me that had that impulse.

The adult remained a good distance.

"Mama, is that you?" Apollonia asked in Greek. "But it cannot be. You have eyes like..." Her voice trailed off as if she finished her thought in her head or lost track of what she was thinking. If it weren't for the shadows where eyes should be, Apollonia could be mistaken for an Olympian. She was that gorgeous. I cleared my throat, nowhere near removing the lump there.

"Yaya isn't here, mama. It's me, Lydia."

My voice was smaller, weaker than I'd like, annoying me. I've done plenty of things in my life. Why was I reduced to a child, wanting her mother's love and approval?

Even though I wanted her to embrace me, to apologize for leaving me behind, and to say all the things I daydreamed of her saying, I mentally prepared for refusal. Of course, she would deny my claim. I wasn't a little girl anymore, but she was a shade and might be stuck in whatever mindset she'd had as a child. A small part of me, a fragile, timid part, expected worse than a denial. Apathy. She abandoned me to be an Oracle. Why would she care that I was here now?

Instead of doing any of these things, my mother took me in, heartbreak limning her gorgeous features. She whispered, "Of course it's you. I've missed so much."

Anger ignited, a small flame among the shards of hurt shredding my heart. However, that flame burned hot. I scoffed. "You've missed it all."

She nodded slowly, her expression mournful.

A mean-spirited piece of me enjoyed that expression. I hurt and wanted to hurt in return.

"I was so young. I thought you'd be better off with—" Apollonia cut herself off and shook her head, dark curls flowing with the movement. Even in her remorse, my mother looked more beautiful than I ever could.

She may be lovely and eternally youthful but what she did to me was ugly. Her abandonment diminished any awe I'd felt looking at her as a child.

She frowned, still looking introspective. "Doesn't matter what I thought. I was a bad mother, abandoning my child for my lover. I knew I didn't belong in Elysium. This is my reckoning."

I exhaled, loudly. I couldn't take the self-pity. She could have apologized, could have explained, but all my mother did was make me the bad guy of her afterlife. To say I was disappointed with this reunion was an understatement. I wanted to be anywhere but here, but I needed her to tell me what happened with the Titans to get her here. "No it isn't. I'm not here for you to do some sort of penance. I'm the new Oracle. I need information only you have."

She backed up a step or two. "Like what?"

Great. Caginess was all I needed. I wondered if she feared I'd ask about my father. She said something about a lover. Could she have left me for my dad? Who was he that she agreed to take on the Oracle position?

"For starters, how did you die?"

Her presence thinned as if the solidness of her drained away a little. "I don't remember."

From years of reading people, that was a straight up lie. She remembered, alright. I wasn't going to get it from her. "What's the last thing you remember?"

Apollonia hugged herself and looked off into the distance, as if she could see the memory on the eternal twilight horizon. "I gave a reading for a Port Angeles local. She was a Neo-Greco-Romanist, who wanted to know about her love life. She left, satisfied because I'd told her she'd find a partner who shared her new faith." Her eyebrows scrunched as she explained, "She was nobody affiliated with Greek heritage or our gods. A lot of people, who were turned off by the whole Paradise Center scandal, were turning to the Olympians or other old pantheons. It's part of your job as Oracle to guide them—" She smiled faintly. "I suppose Dione or Hermes has already told you that."

Pinching my lips tight, I nodded curtly. I would offer her no more since she gave me so little.

"Was the client's name Jen?" I asked. It was a shot in the dark, but maybe Echidna posed as a human to lure Apollonia.

Apollonia's eyebrows crept up and her hand touched her chest. "Yes."

"Was there anything unusual about her?"

"Only that she wore an oversized hat and sunglasses. It was an overcast day. At least I assume so. It often is in Washington." She offered a smile that reminded me so much of my grandmother it hurt. "Hope you can get used to that. Took me a bit."

I found myself smiling back. Catching myself, I wiped the smile from my face. I hated that my heart lapped up that little nugget of warmth. How pathetic was I that I still wanted a mother so badly that I let her thin gesture mean anything? I could see Carlo shaking his head. He'd taught me better than that. This woman abandoned me, probably for some hot god or whatever, and now wanted to bond because she was dead and regretful. Too bad. She wasn't going to get love or forgiveness from me.

"Which god did you abandon me for?"

Apollonia recoiled as if struck. Then she jutted out her chin, showing some of my grandfather's pride. "No *god*. I am—I was a lesbian."

I pointed to myself, as demonstration that she'd been with at least one dude. "Um? Immaculate conception or invitro?"

My mother laughed. "I didn't say I was exclusive to cisgender women, my daughter. Besides, in the supernatural world, you'll find a lot more...variety. You'd be surprised."

Not wanting to go down that road with my *mother*, I asked, "Who then, Apollonia?"

"She is known by a few names. Aello, Nicothoë, Podarge. I called her Nicky."

I remembered the names from my grandparent's stories. Aello was a harpy or a wind spirit, and none of the stories about her shed a flattering light. Who she was now or what she had to do with my mother's demise, remained to be seen.

"Did Nicky meet Jen?"

Apollonia shook her head. "No. I kept my Oracle duties and my household with Nicky separate. I became the Oracle to live as long as my love." She sighed. "How disappointing to give up everything to not live as long as my mortal lifespan would've granted."

"Yeah. Too bad."

If she wanted pity from me, she'd get none. My grandparents were elderly and had to care for a child. The added expense and responsibility likely didn't help their mortal lifespan, not that this woman cared. How bizarre to see someone who looked so much like the person from the photographs and yet be so different than the person I heard so much about.

"When I made my choice, I was a teenager, Lydia. How much perspective did you have at that age?"

Not much, or I wouldn't have ended up in bed with Carlo let alone married him. I kept those details to myself. Apollonia died in an unfortunate way, but she hadn't lived in a way that gave her the right to know me. Instead of replying to her baiting, I asked, "Is there anything you can tell me that might help?"

"Hera is a jealous bitch. If she learns the truth, you won't live long."

"What truth?"

Apollonia's thinning form flickered like a glitching hologram. A golden bird-woman with her face, at least seven feet tall, stood in her place. Then she was my mother again, or at least the human-looking person that had given birth to me. The shade shook her head slowly, confusion twisting her features. She gripped her hair at the sides of her head, her form flickering.

"I can't remember."

"That's all we need, Apollonia," Persephone soothed, linking her arm with mine. "Rest."

CHAPTER
TWENTY

Persephone waited while I gathered my belongings. Rattled, I took my time.

"Ready?" the goddess asked.

Not feeling like talking, I nodded.

"Remember to call him Spot outside of Hades." Persephone handed me a leash with the three-headed Cerberus attached to the other end.

I debated for a moment whether I should take the pooch, but I also didn't want to end up pulled in another direction by another Titan, siren, fae, or god. Being over forty years old, I wanted to make my own path as much as possible within the confines of this bizarre situation, please and thank you. My new monster doggo would at least help with that.

Persephone did some hand-waving, magical stuff I wasn't paying too close of attention to. Cerberus's nearest head was chewing on the toe of my shoe, and I was doing my best to deter him from doing it. Leave it to me to get an untrained demon dog as a pet protector.

Smoke swirled in a circle from floor to ceiling. It reeked of sulfur and iron. Not pleasant at all. The smoke dissipated, revealing the train car as I'd left it frozen in time.

The queen of the underworld squeezed my arm, her eyes luminescent and eyebrows pinched. "I'm sorry your reunion with your mother wasn't as you'd hoped it would be."

"Me too."

"I will keep speaking to her, drawing out the memory so we know exactly how she died."

I nodded, not committing to any sentiment about it.

"Did she mention who your father was?"

I shook my head.

"Something she's kept the secret your whole life, even from Olympus." She glanced at the window. "Perhaps they were merely human but knowing my kin they were likely someone not of your world. The gods love bedding and wedding mortals." She looked off wistfully and then gave me a rueful smile. "There is something to be said of a fleeting life and the urgency of it."

"I guess if I don't stick my neck out, mine won't be fleeting." I was thinking about the whole immortality clause.

The goddess made a non-committal shrug and then gestured to the train.

I returned to the car, luggage and Hades doggo in tow. Then I turned for one last look at the beautiful queen and her palace.

"If anyone asks, Cerberus came to you," Persephone said with a wink and a grin. "It's important everyone believes that you didn't seek my assistance."

"Technically, he did," I replied, smiling back. "And I didn't."

Smoke filled the hole between worlds. The lights flickered and the train started again. I almost fell with the sudden movement. Cerberus nudged me straight.

Or, rather, a large black lab named Spot. As if I would forget his name, he had a thick red leather collar with the name in English embossed in gold letters.

"Well, I guess it's just you and me."

When we reached the stop, Cerberus and I got off with no officers or meddlesome nymphs in sight. A starry night canopied the parking lot that seemed to stretch on as far as the fields of asphodel in the Underworld. I scanned the lot for taxis or car services but there appeared to be none.

"Guess we'll have to hoof it for a bit, Spot."

Cerberus panted and stared at me blankly.

"Or should I say paw and foot it?" I laughed at my own joke.

The guardian of Hades drooled.

Right. Now I was talking to dogs as if they were intelligent beings with decision capabilities beyond eat, poop, mate, and sleep.

Fine.

I decided to head in what seemed to be due west, weaving my way through the lot. Cerberus didn't give me too many problems. He was actually helpful, nudging me away from people and certain areas. I didn't fuss, trusting he knew who and what was good for me. Besides, fighting a giant monster had already been scratched off my to-do list this week. I'd rather go with the flow.

At length I found signage for a terminal where shuttles took people to a rental car facility. I had a license—technically six licenses altogether—from various states. With Carlo on the run from the law, I didn't dare use my license with the same last name. I rummaged through my purse while waiting for the bus, deciding to be Penelope from Pennsylvania. "Penny" was a middle-aged housewife with not too much credit because her Eagles football-team-loving, Jeep-driving husband only allowed her a limited card.

The driver of the shuttle, a man in his early sixties reeking of aftershave, sneered at Cerberus. "It needs crate."

"Spot is a service dog," I preempted, hoping he wouldn't ask why there was no vest saying so. "Highly trained."

The driver grunted something and took one of my suitcases. Dispute over, I guess. I held on to the one with my grandparents' stuff and settled in a seat with Cerberus at my feet. About an hour later, I had procured a rental, directions to an all-night diner, and an old-fashioned map to guide me to Seattle.

After getting Cerberus and I some grub at the diner, I drove until my eyelids got heavy. Then, I drove for a bit more until found a rest stop. There, I let Cerberus out to do his doggy business while I used the facilities.

He waited for me by the entrance, dead jack rabbit in his maw.

"Gobble it up or spit it out. That's not going in the rental."

His head shook side to side, blurring until three monstrous heads appeared. The three heads went to work, shredding and devouring his prey with gusto.

Unable to stomach the live-action Animal Planet, I went to wait in the car. Not long after, the erstwhile monster appeared as a docile black lab. I let him in and lowered my seat to nap.

"Keep watch until I wake up," I commanded, since he seemed to understand me the last time. "Don't eat anyone unless I say so, got me?"

Cerberus woofed.

"I'll take that as a yes."

The pooch settled in on the passenger seat, staring out the front window. With a monster who looked like an innocent black lab on guard duty, I drifted off to sleep.

CHAPTER

TWENTY-ONE

After days of turmoil, a couple of quiet days on the road got monotonous. Yeah, the mountains and high desert had some amazing vistas, but driving got old. I took a lot of rest stops, letting Cerberus hunt, and feeding him hotdogs and burgers from gas stations.

The pseudo-Lab would eat a frank that had been under a hot lamp for hours, or whatever vermin he could scrounge, but turned his nose up at a bag of dry dog food. He even had the nerve to look offended that I'd tried to serve him kibble! Which was bizarre, considering he also ate a lot of non-foods that ended up causing extra stops for whatever he hurled. Sometimes he puked more than whole crushed cans, bones of his prey, fur, and so much nasty things that I didn't want to think about. Then the genius would try to lap up whatever his body evacuated as if it would go down better the second time around.

After pushing Cerberus out of the car for the billionth time to clean up another pile of puke, I began to wonder if Persephone lent me a guardian of Hades or got rid of her husband's moron pet. If someone were taking bets, I'd put all my money on the latter.

Done cleaning, I watched the Underworld dog sprint past the rest stop building to a creek. I ruminated on the information I'd gathered from my mother and what had happened over the days prior. ruminated.

Echidna, or Jen as I called her, had come to my mom as a client. Echidna had come to me as well. For some reason, they didn't kill me. Everyone speculated that she and Typhon wanted to open Tartarus using an oracle, but nobody was wondering why they'd killed my mother. It made no sense to kill her. She was the key to opening Tartarus. Did they exsanguinate her for some sort of ritual that would open the gates?

I shuddered and dismissed the possibility. I'd seen a few shades who had obvious stab wounds or other injuries. My mother had seemed...whole.

Why did Echidna say that "the key" was safe? Did I assume the wrong thing and that she hadn't meant me or had she only been reassuring me so that I wouldn't give her any problems?

So many unanswered questions. I was good at reading people and figuring out how to give them advice on their problems. If I took away Echidna and Typhon's monster appearance and made them Jen and Brad in my mind, would I think that they intentionally killed my mom?

Probably not.

Besides, it made no sense to kill her if they needed her.

It made more sense that someone who didn't want them to succeed killed her and made it look like the monsters did it. Since no one on Olympus wanted them to succeed that meant it could be anyone.

I ruled out Zeus. He would have just killed me after he learned what he wanted to. I also ruled out Hermes. The messenger seemed genuinely relieved he'd found me alive in Miriam's faerie. Also, he saved me twice. It would have been easier to let me die in that fire when I was a kid than to save me.

Cerberus returned; head tilted to one side.

"I'm just trying to figure out who my enemies are. Want some lunchmeat?"

The pseudo-black lab pointed his nose toward the door. That was a no, and he wanted to leave now. I obliged, letting him in. He hopped in the passenger seat, circled once and then settled.

I closed the door and got in on the driver's side. My nose itched, so I flipped down the visor to see if I'd rubbed something nasty on myself while cleaning dog vomit. There was nothing on my nose. Just an itch. However, my gaze caught my eyes.

They weren't like my grandparents or my mother's eyes. Not that her eyes were the same anymore, but I'd seen plenty of pictures.

"Where did you come from?"

Cerberus nudged my arm with a slobbery maw.

After a couple days of getting drooled on I was no longer phased by the wetness. I scratched between his ears. "You're right, Spot. I'm not going to get answers here."

After starting up the car, I pulled out of the lot. I made good time, eating a lot of highway. Much later, I took an exit to get gas.

I caught my reflection in the rearview mirror at a four-way stop. I stared in the mirror. My mother's pronouncement about Hera being jealous played in my head. I pulled over in a nearby lot and dug into my purse.

The dog watched me, and scanned the lot for whatever, in turns.

"Watch my stuff. There's someone I need to talk to. I'll let you out when I get back."

Cerberus woofed.

"Thanks."

After I shut the door behind me, I paused and palmed my face. Next, I'll be interpreting Cerberus's barks as sentences. Call me Timmy and Cerberus, my personal Underworld monster Lassie.

It was late in the evening. The parking lot had few cars and patrons, which would make my purpose easier. Maybe the Seattle supernaturals ripped open the veil between mundane and the magical, but I didn't need to draw undue attention. What I was about to attempt would freak out a passerby.

I made my way to the intersection. Standing on the corner, I held the coin Hermes gave me between my fingers and rubbed the metal, hoping the god would come. Technically, my life really was in peril since the Titans wanted to use me in a way that would kill me—just not in peril at the moment.

It didn't work.

These sleepy towns didn't have much traffic after that time. I decided to risk going in the center of the crossroads.

"Hermes," I shouted at the top of my lungs, my voice cracking with distress. I'd been shipped around between the Underworld, a faerie, Olympus, and the Underworld again in only a few days. I had Titans or gods who wanted to either use me or kill me.

In my periphery, a light flashed. Cerberus let out a sound that was half battle howl, half roar. I spun around, running to save my dog. As I ran toward the battle, it *should* have occurred to me, if Cerberus couldn't fight off whatever it was *I* sure couldn't.

I found the hound atop a prone Hermes. The pooch swung his three heads in my direction, panting and eyes bright. His doggy mug had an expression that asked, "Am I a good boy?"

"What a good boy, Spot," I cooed. In a firm tone, I added, "Now let him go."

Cerberus whined but relented, transforming to a happy black lab and settling at my side.

Hermes pushed onto his hands and feet, shaking his head like a dog shaking off water. His wings flexed. There seemed to be damage to one. Golden sparks ignited in the affected area, burning in a warm glow until the damage repaired itself.

Neat trick.

"Sorry my dog attacked you." I bit my lip, worried the god would try to fight Cerberus again.

Hermes rose to his full height, eyes blazing. Literally. Fire replaced his eyeballs. The effect made me cringe. His whole body shook with rage. "Why did you leave Olympus without telling me?"

"I didn't leave on my own volition."

"Are you telling me that my own eyes, that the whole court of Olympus didn't see you walk out of the throne room with Thetis?" The god's arm shot out. "That you're not standing right here, right now no one's prisoner."

"Is that what happened?"

The bonfires dimmed to regular eyes, though his brows remained knitted together and his arms folded tightly across his chest. "What do you mean?"

"I become disoriented and confused after a vision," I told him, not willing to admit the lights were on but nobody was home when I had visions.

He stroked his chin, anger melting into curiosity. "I have known many oracles. None have mentioned this effect before. Perhaps this is an affliction?"

I hesitated. Should I admit that I'm not in control when I have visions? Was this something all oracles hid? I smiled. "Well, an oracle tells all for everyone else. Don't you think she'd like to keep some secrets of her own?"

Hermes considered it for a moment. "It would be wise not to share this with others—if you didn't leave Olympus of your own accord, how did you get here?"

I explained waking up on a plane with who I assume was Thetis, but who appeared human. How she sprayed something in my face and how I woke again in an airport then rented the car. Leaving out that I'd been to Hades seemed like a giant gap, but I'd promised Persephone.

"How did you come across Cer—"

I pressed my finger to his lips to quiet him. "Shh! Call him Spot."

At first, his eyes widened. Then, a slow grin spread on Hermes mouth. Something about the god changed, a softening of all his features and his body. His gaze fell.

My gaze dipped to where his fell on my finger still pressed against his grinning lips. When I returned to his eyes, so much warmth and tenderness awaited me there.

My heart threatened to pound out of my chest. I didn't know why he looked at me like that. We didn't know each other. I pulled back a step. Cerberus growled behind me, warning Hermes not to come closer.

"Cool it," I chided over my shoulder.

Cerberus stopped growling, but his doggy stare remained fixed on Hermes.

Okay.

I took a deep breath. "He found me on the train. I couldn't just leave him there."

Hermes looked past me at the dog. "That beast is Persephone's hound. My sibling is an Olympian, but her loyalties lie with Hades and the dog's loyalties lie with her. Don't ever mistake him as yours. He's a spy."

Uh huh. Lots of secret agents ate soap, vomited it, and lapped it up again. Very James Bond.

"Isn't it his job to guard Tartarus?"

"Yes." The god drew out the word, hesitant likely because it wasn't obvious where I was going with the question.

"Then wouldn't it make sense that he would find the person the Titans want to use to open Tartarus and guard that person?"

He scratched the back of his head. "I suppose, but—"

Faster than I could track, faster than my brain could comprehend, Hermes snatched me around the waist and pulled me through cold and darkness into a small meadow. Full daylight and brilliant blue sky shone above. Mountains surrounded us.

"What the heck?" I pushed him trying to flee his embrace, but I might as well have pushed a cement wall. "Let me go!"

His face was implacable and his grip like an iron band. "Powerful forces fight over your existence. Some on Olympus want you dead, thinking that will stop the prophecy you made. I have no patience for falsehoods. I am your protector, willed so by my father. I have watched you your entire life, seeing to your safety. It wasn't easy. You did not lead the life of a girl in a small mountain village like your ancestors. So, when I warn you that beast is not your friend and a spy, I'd like you to consider I may be right. At least consider."

Well, that was a lot to unpack. I had my own personal stalker. I felt like asking why he let me marry Carlo, but I knew the answer. He wasn't allowed to interfere with my life, he was only tasked with protecting me—or some nonsense like that. Abuse came in a lot of forms. Why were people only concerned with the physical kind?

Was Hermes the reason Carlo could burn a lot of bridges with dangerous people and get away with it? I'd worried many nights about when his enemies would come for me or Lukie. Maybe Hermes had stopped them.

"I tell you what. If you tell me who my father is, I'll consider it."

The god blinked. His grip loosened, but only slightly. Lips pressed tight, Hermes's exhale whooshed out his nostrils. "I don't know. Apollonia had quite a few lovers before she settled with Nicky."

"None of them were from Olympus?"

His brows furrowed. "Why do you ask?"

I didn't reply right away. I couldn't tell him I'd talked to Apollonia without telling him about my encounter with Persephone. "Hera showed up in your room. She had a particular interest in me." I held up my hands, the only free part of me, and wiggled my fingers. "Also, I can zap people."

He revealed straight, white teeth. "We don't share a father. I would know if Zeus trod in that direction. The King of the Olympians is not subtle when someone becomes the object of his desire."

I swallowed hard, afraid of Zeus swinging any attention my way. "Good to know."

Sifting his fingers through my curls, the handsome god added, "There's something else you should know."

The way he looked at me reminded me of the way men looked at me when I was young and attractive. Maybe I was still attractive? I'd played the role of Francine Lawless, wife, mom, and fake medium for so long, I'd forgotten who Lydia Kourakos was and how she felt.

"What's that?" I asked, breathless.

"Neither am I."

The kiss that followed was a press of flesh against flesh, no tongue, no teeth, but my toes curled in my shoes and my knees turned to jelly. A stifled moan emitted from my throat.

I'd read The Princess Bride to Luke when he was a child. He'd gotten sick of Greek myths and wanted something else. I liked the movie, so I got the book. Luke and I loved the book, and the movie even more. The movie described the kiss between Buttercup and Wesley in a way that seemed utterly romantic and completely implausible.

This kiss was better.

TWENTY-TWO

When Hermes and I returned to the rental, Cerberus growled. The protective monster pooch was concerned about my sudden disappearance, I suppose. I spun around, demonstrating that I was unharmed.

The growl intensified and his Labrador Retriever guise wavered. If I looked just so, I could see the larger, three-headed version under the illusion. Maybe Cerberus just didn't like the god getting more Lydia time, or maybe Hermes made him look bad at his spy/guard dog job, if he was somehow reporting back to Persephone.

"Shut your trap, or no gas station hotdogs for you," I warned, shaking my finger at the supernatural pooch.

The Underworld guardian quieted, except for a whimper of protest, as if he were saying that he was only doing his job. Guess the pooch did listen to me. Or the monster really loved hotdogs. Who knew?

"I'm fine," I assured him. Remembering what Hermes said about spying, I added, "Why don't you hunt for a bit?"

Cerberus's muzzle whipped in the direction of some trees

bordering the lot and then back to me and Hermes. The dog gave the god a warning look, and then trotted off.

"I don't think the Titans killed my mother," I confessed. "I don't think they were going to harm me either."

His brow creased, but he didn't dismiss my theory right away. "What makes you think that?"

How much should I tell him? I wasn't loyal to Persephone, per se. She might be involving herself for the self-interest of protecting Tartarus, but giving me a chance to see my mother again didn't benefit her at all. I trusted my gut with her, too. She seemed to truly care what happened to my mother's shade. At least enough to bring her to the borders of Elysium and the Asphodel Fields of Hades. Only those related to the gods and heroes belonged there.

"You said it yourself. Olympus debates my existence. Maybe someone felt that way about my mother and got to her before the Titans could use her?"

Hermes scoffed. "No. Apollonia was cherished by Olympus as an excellent oracle. No one would harm her."

"So, I come with bad news, and everyone wants me dead?"

I crossed my arms over my chest, suddenly cold. Maybe jail would have been better than being hunted down by gods. Not that jail would protect me from that hunt.

"I like you." His chest puffed out. "I'll protect you."

I fought the urge to roll my eyes. The overprotective god, who stalked me my whole life because it was his job, was not what I needed from Hermes right now—or ever, really. I could handle myself. I had handled myself against Titans and the nymph.

"Thetis wanted to get rid of me. Who is she working for, Zeus?"

"No. Father had been perturbed you'd disappeared."

I remembered the water nymph in Hermes bathroom and Hera's warning.

"Hera said that all the nymphs were Zeus's creatures." She also said Zeus would want to seduce me, but I kept that to myself. "I don't get it. Why would Thetis kidnap me if Zeus hadn't told her to do so?"

"Nymphs can have minds of their own and reasons of their own for doing things." Stroking his chin, Hermes grimaced. "I don't like that Hera said that about the nymphs. They are not my father's creatures. My mother was a nymph and may have been Zeus's lover, but Maia was never his tool."

"Was the nymph in your bathroom your mom?"

He shook his head mournfully. "You cannot meet my mother."

His expression shifted. A smile crept up on his lips. The glow of pride illuminated his face. "That was my sister. I told her to look after you. I'm glad you met."

I don't know why but I liked that it was his sister not some random nymph lurking about his bathroom. "Oh, darn. I wish Hera wouldn't have made her leave. I'd have loved to get to know your sister."

Hermes's grin faded. "The queen seeking you out privately is concerning. My father may have had an eye for your line in the beginning while he had his time with Dione, but he's never shown any special interest in oracles in thousands of years on your world. The only reason why he wanted a prediction from you was because I told him that two Titans had escaped. He has no designs on you, especially after that prophecy. He wouldn't admit it, but you frightened him."

I wished I knew what that prophecy was.

"I only told them what I saw," I guessed. I didn't make it up. I couldn't if I wasn't aware of the prophecy at all.

"They can't control the future." Hermes shrugged. "So the gods will focus on what they *can* control."

I rubbed my arms. "Me?"

He nodded. His eyes had pity I didn't want in them. "Don't trust anything that comes from Hera's lips. She's a jealous, vengeful goddess."

"I don't trust anyone," I told him.

"You can trust me, I swear it," Hermes vowed, face earnest.

My skin prickled and warmth sunk deep inmy flesh. A vow of a god was binding. I knew that much from my grandparents' stories.

He plucked a coin out of thin air, handing it to me.

I took it and asked, "I need two now?"

"The other will need a bit before it will work again."

I grinned. "Does it need to charge its magical batteries?"

He responded with a thousand-watt smile. "Yes. Exactly."

"If you're my protector, why do you come and go?"

The smile dropped. "I cannot stay in this world for long. No god can."

"Because it isn't meant for immortals?"

The hard line of his jaw tightened and a muscle in his sculpted cheek feathered. "There was a time when gods of the flesh could roam this world when they pleased, sometimes for a span of more than one human lifetime. This was in a time before kings decided a small but growing cult of monotheism would give them more power than the old gods." In a soft and mournful voice, he added, "And our chaos."

I reached my hand to touch his. Though Greece welcomed many religions, the Eastern Orthodox church was part of the national identity. The monks of the religion kept the language and history alive, fleeing to the caves of Meteora. There they hid in caves and later built full monasteries on the high altitudes of the rock formations during the Turkish occupation.

Resolve settled into his features. He squared his shoulders. His golden wings unfurled, spanning at least six feet on either side before they dissolved into white wisps of smoke and then nothing at all. The god gestured to my rental car. "I will accompany you for a while. There are things you must know."

CHAPTER
TWENTY-THREE

After he'd been my navigator for so long, convincing Cerberus to sit in the back, proved more difficult than escaping Titans. The monster pooch finally relented after I got a pack of uncooked hotdogs from the trunk, dumped the whole thing in his dog bowl, and placed it on the back seat. With the monster doggo chomping in the back, I got in the front.

After I started the car, an alert dinged, signaling that Hermes wasn't buckled in. I stretched my own seatbelt. "You'll need to wear one of these."

"Why?"

I cocked my head to the side, wondering if he was joking but his expression was earnest. "It's a seatbelt, it's for your protection."

"If I cannot withstand whatever this meager strap of material would protect me from, I might as well be a mortal." Every word dripped with his indignation. "It is not necessary."

I pinched the bridge of my nose. Giving up, I put the car in drive and turned on the radio to drown out the incessant dinging. I found a 90s pop station. Ace of Base's "I Saw the Sign" played. Just perfect.

"Why is your transportation making that awful noise? It's ruining the delightful tune."

"Because you won't wear your seatbelt, Hermes."

He strapped himself in, smiling. "You should've said so earlier. That's much better."

I THOUGHT the Messenger of the Gods would have verbally vomited the deets on Olympus right away, but he took in his surroundings making idle chit chat. He commented on the steady pace of the car being soothing but not as fast as he'd like.

I'd had fortune seeker clients who behaved like this. Unless they were in emotional duress, they had to talk a bit before addressing their issues. Some of them needed a licensed therapist, and I'd guide them that way. Some needed a friend to listen without judgment, who would offer unbiased advice that leaned toward what they wanted to do anyway.

After a period of extended silence, Hermes began, "Since humans crawled from the depths of Poseidon's domain and stood on two legs like a god, they held a magic no other creature possessed."

Having two storyteller grandparents, I knew this was the point where I was supposed to participate with a guess. I would say imagination, but all sentient beings had that. Then I thought about what gods craved and what men wanted: worship and admiration. There was a kind of power in that.

"Belief?"

"Correct. Belief has always been known to drive the gods' power beyond what we're born with or assert over their will. Some gods become so powerful they can no longer exist within the framework of this world or many others. They are called many things, I prefer the term ascended. To reach this state of being is the goal of many gods." He chuckled. "Well, those not so tied to their flesh as Olympians."

I glanced at him. A grin that was at once sly and rueful touched his lips. He had the most expressive face. I could watch it for hours. Unfortunately, I had to keep my eyes on the road. Interstate driving at night could get monotonous, but I still needed to stay in my lane. Veering off into the brush would be nothing compared to what I've endured this trip, but I'd had enough excitement.

"We didn't see it coming. The cult was laughable to us. We'd seen so many rise and fall. The Abrahamic religions weren't new, either. Much of their notions of a god were based on Zeus. Olympians had helped the Greeks, and later the Romans, create great civilizations modeled after our own world. We'd underestimated zealous belief. The angels grew in power in what was a blink of an eye of our long existence. Instead of one generation overpowering the other, like the Olympians ridding the multiverse of Titans, we were replaced by a god we'd thought was a trend and would only be a flash in our long existence. A god, who gained so much belief so quickly, he's already ascended."

In my periphery, he clenched his fist, his gaze somewhere far away.

"So foolish in our hubris."

I laid my free hand over his. "You're not omnipotent. How could you know?"

At that moment, our gazes met. So many different emotions churned. A storm gathered in his dark eyes.

"The Oracle warned us Emperor Constantine would change everything. Do you know what my father said?"

There was no way I could, but I shook my head anyway.

"He'll die. This empire will crumble. Multi-theism will return. He was right, but in that time we weakened. Olympus had to bow to beings lesser than gods just to survive. We sip from the modicum of belief gained by our stories told over and over. We cannot stay here on Earth for long." He blew out his breath. His gaze far away. "My extended presence here is against the treaty with the Angelic Anocracy, but I don't care. The angels won't come in Gabriel Crowfoot's territory. That nephil-shifter scares them. I wish a nephil like him had come about sooner. I wish someone, *anyone* had the nerve to defy the angels before."

"Why didn't the Olympians? You're gods."

"Our magic, our realms have weakened so significantly that Titans have escaped Tartarus."

Cerberus whined.

Hermes reached back, consoling the paranormal pup with ear scritches. "It's not your fault. You're not what you once were." More quietly, he added, "None of us are."

I knew the feeling. It wasn't the same as losing power as a god, but I'd once been young, smart, and strong. I'd had a mind that was sharper than everyone I'd met. Now, I go into a room and forget what I came in for. I was slower and rounder, less agile. My body handed me a list of complaints at the end of each day, sometimes not waiting until I shuffled into bed and plowed my face into a pillow before various parts screamed, "I hurt!" Not only that, at one point I'd been my husband and son's sun, moon, and stars. They both eventually took all my little labors of love for granted. I could forgive Luke. He needed to sprout wings and fly away from the Neverland and his father's Lost Boys crew. Carlo, on the other hand, began to feel entitled to my time, my heart, and my money, and it showed. Then, he couldn't care less if I existed. He'd once called me 'roomie' in front of his friends.

The jabs and the responding laughter often echoed in my head.

"Getting old and forgotten sucks," I said with a heavy sigh.

"You are young and beautiful with a long life ahead of you, if I can help it."

I open my mouth to explain what I mean, not that I wanted to share that shame with a flawless god, but I wanted him to understand how I related. Before I could form the words clearly, he spoke again.

"I've watched you long enough to know you mean that silly boy who you kept company with lost interest. Carlo is a fool. He had greatness in front of him and threw away what some men would kill and die for, and for what? Nothing of consequence."

Warmth bloomed in my face and chest, concentrating mostly on my cheeks. Probably a hot flash. I was in my forties after all.

"You should take on a lover. Someone experienced, who will provide you with much pleasure and cherish you for all that you are."

I scoffed. "Yeah right. Not at my age, Hermes."

He turned toward me fully with a note of command in his voice, when he said, "Pull the vehicle to the side of the road."

I did as he asked, turning the engine off when I did. Guess this was the end of having a companion that didn't bark or puke every five minutes. It was nice while it lasted.

"Get out of the car." He turned to Cerberus, who was fast asleep. "We won't be long. Stay."

My chest tightened as I got out and walked around the front. I didn't know how much I wanted a companion until I didn't have one.

Hermes met me in the light of the head beams, offering a hand.

I took it, heart racing.

I could usually read a person to know what's going to happen next, but his face and body language remained neutral. It didn't take much to get out of the light of my vehicle and into the darkness running parallel to the deserted highway.

"Look up."

I did as he asked, gasping at the sight.

No monsters, no gods, only a sea of stars and beautiful bright patches of color, the nebulae. Born and living in the cities of the Eastern seaboard, I'd never seen the night sky like this. Not in real life.

"Take a deep breath."

I did. I could smell the dirt under our feet, something wet not far off, maybe a stream, and Hermes' distinct scent. Soothing heat rolled of something nearby. My heart fluttered with the understanding that he was standing close again.

"Look at me."

I did as he asked again. Why not? Everything else had been pleasant.

"You are the wonder, Lydia, not I. No one in the entirety of existence is like you and no one ever will be. You are better than Carlo in every way. He will come to regret his treatment of you. Every person who did not see what stood before them soon will. I see you. The adoring mother, the confidante and advisor to many, and the Oracle with other magics that she shouldn't possess, yet you do. Olympus needs you, not the other way around. Remember that."

Unsure of what to say, I nodded.

"Do you want to be kissed?"

I blinked. "I—uh—"

I wanted to be kissed. I missed the days of wanting and being wanted.

I grinned. "Do you want to kiss me again, Hermes?"

"Yes, Lydia." Hermes smiled. "Very much so."

Despite not feeling nonchalant at all, I shrugged. "Okay. Let's kiss."

He no longer looked like an impossibly handsome *man*. His skin radiated a magenta light with silvery flecks. His golden wings sprouted and unfurled, fanning out behind him. Hermes wanted me to see him as he truly appeared.

An arm in possession of perfectly sculpted muscle snaked its way around my waist, pulling my soft and squishy flesh against his hard body.

I squeaked.

He grinned as he lowered his head, but his eyes were all molten heat.

I hadn't ever had anyone look at me like that, not even when I had youth on my side. The desire in his eyes livened up places that needed a few cobwebs knocked down.

He stopped just before our lips met. His gaze scanned my face. Hermes must have seen what he was looking for because his mouth again found mine.

CHAPTER

TWENTY-FOUR

After everything he'd said, I'd assumed Hermes would return to Olympus. He didn't leave me. He walked me back to the car and got in, too. Well, he walked, and I *floated* back. The kiss helped my mood. It was nice to be wanted after years of rejection, even self-rejection.

I always thought Carlo and I had grown apart because I'd gotten older, a little rounder and wasn't the bright-eyed, smiling girl that my ex fell in love with anymore, but the problem wasn't me. My husband had held me to an impossible standard because he didn't even meet the bare minimum of a good man. He'd made me feel undesirable.

A god kissed me. A god wanted me. Part of me wished Carlo could've seen it. I would love to be petty and rub it into his face. Another part loved that he didn't know. That he went about thinking I was floundering without him, maybe even in jail for his crimes.

I drove another hour before Hermes pointed out an exit ahead. "There's a motel on that road. It's clean and inexpensive, not to mention safe. Let's go there and rest for the night."

Until that night I'd been sleeping in the car. I looked over my shoulder. "Do they take pets?"

Hermes chuckled. "Cer—Spot can sleep in the car."

Cerberus lifted his head, shook it and then went back to sleep.

Shortly after, Hermes, suddenly clothed in t-shirt and gray sweatpants, accompanied me into the office of a motel.

The office itself was interesting. A small space with a myriad of intricately woven tapestries covering every inch of the walls. Several hand-woven rugs covered the floor. The waiting area sofa had doilies on the arms and afghans piled on the back and more spread over the cushions. The sole chair also had doilies and afghans.

Even as a granddaughter of a weaver, I thought this was overkill.

A woman in her late sixties, possibly early seventies, sat behind the front desk. A pink muumuu with blue flowers draped generously over her rotund frame. Rotund wasn't an accurate description. She had spindly arms and a thin upper body but seemed to be suffering some sort of edema condition where her lower half swelled far beyond what should be proportionate to her upper body. Curlers of the same color as her dress peeked from underneath an electric blue scarf with matching pink roses, wrapping her silver hair. Yellowing brown eyes covered in thick, cat-eye framed glasses peered at us from behind a desk. Her red knitting needles, working on an afghan-in-progress, kept clicking.

"You two don't look like you're from around here. Lost, are you?" She had more of a folksy accent than the southern drawl I was used to, but I knew country poor when I heard it.

I opened my mouth to speak, but Hermes spoke first.

"I'm never lost, and you know it, Arachne," Hermes said in Greek.

The needles ceased clicking. The elderly woman lowered her afghan-in-progress and straightened. Her body made awful popping and cracking sounds with the movement. Perhaps she was older than her seventies.

"So, Olympus has found me. I knew nothing good would come of the veil between mundane and supernatural being lifted."

Hermes held his hands up. "I'm not here as herald. I'm here as a person in need of rest in a safe space. I know no better guardian than you."

Arachne sniffed the air. "Is that so? I smell a far fiercer creature than I."

"Spot is mine," I offer. "He won't harm you as long as you don't harm me."

The elderly woman laughed, a brittle sound. "I'm not the one that started the harm, but no, Spot, as you call him, won't bother me none." She transitioned once again into her folksy English. "His original owner set me up here."

She gestured in a wide sweep, indicating the motel office.

I knew Arachne's story but not that ending. My grandmother, a former weaver, loved to tell it. Arachne herself was a weaver from the city I was named after, Lydia. She and Athena got into a weaving contest. Arachne wove better. Athena, Goddess of Wisdom and Crafts, grew angry over a mere mortal out-weaving her. She beat Arachne. Distraught, the poor weaver took her own life, turning into a spider after her death. The moral of the story was to not outdo a god who gave you a gift in the first place. I thought gods were petty and cruel to be jealous of humans.

She set her afghan-in-progress on the counter, then rose. There was something off about the way she rose. She got straight up instead of scooting off a chair and up. I didn't hear a scrape against the floor, indicating the chair was behind her ample bottom half. It was as if the chair disappeared.

Arachne grabbed a key from the wall behind her. A clicking noise, akin to acrylic nails tapping on tile, accompanied the movement. "Normally, I just give guests a key, but I'll walk you to the room to see if it's suitable."

Where did the chair go?

Just when my brain couldn't let go of the question, Arachne rounded the counter.

Seated, the elderly hotel manager gave the impression of a large lower body starting around mid-abdomen, but my brain had filled in *human* legs. Clicking delicately on the floor, eight spindly *spider* legs supported the misshapen form of Arachne.

Horror accompanied the realization that the weaver from Lydia didn't turn into a normal spider. It was as if her human upper body was superglued to a nightmare-sized spider body. The worst part about it was that I couldn't see the spider part except for the legs. The oversized muumuu covered it all in bright pink.

The room shrank and the floor buckled with Arachne's approach.

Air. I needed more air. I gulped it like a woman dying of dehydration gulps water. I turned and bolted out the door.

Outside, an eighteen-wheeler pulled up.

Hyperventilating, I inhaled a cloud of noxious exhaust. Everything spun. The sidewalk tilted.

Cerberus barked from somewhere far away.

I lost balance. My stomach flew into my throat as I surely would kiss pavement in a few seconds. Before I hit the ground, an iron band wrapped around my torso and arms.

Hermes pulled me to him just as the vision pulled me under.

I WALKED behind the witch in a cavern lit by glowing stalactites and stalagmites. My heart raced. I concentrated on the swish of her blue wool skirt, echoed by mine with each tentative step. I wouldn't have dared enter such a place on my own. The boys of my village herded the sheep. The girls stuck to the houses; weaving, cooking, and caring for the children. What would the village elders think of me if they knew what I had been doing? Would the priest call me a heretic? It didn't matter. I would save them all.

"The trial will take only once," the witch said over her shoulder. "Then the gods will accept you as the Oracle."

I nodded, wringing my trembling hands. I wanted to pray to the saints or the Blessed Virgin for courage, but neither Mary nor any saint had saved the rest of my country from the invaders. News came every day about Greeks dying at the hands of the Turks. Men and their greed. We all suffered the consequences.

If the old gods accepted me and gave me the gift of sight, they'd help my people. It was blasphemy. I would go to Hell for calling upon the Olympians, but I would do what I had to do to save my village and my family.

We came to a column made of pure obsidian. Light sparked off the smooth, black surface. Energy vibrated through me like the beat of a drum. I believe it came from the obsidian column.

I lifted my fingers to make the sign of the cross.

The witch spun around, her long hair freeing from its braid. She was more beautiful than anyone I'd ever seen in my life, even for her advanced age. Now, all that beauty slipped like a mask, replaced by wrath. Her features were sharper, twisted with inhuman rage and something not of this world limned her skin. "None of that here!"

I stepped back, as afraid of the unnatural glow in her eyes as much as her sharp tongue.

Something about my fear must have placated the witch. Her eyes still glowed with the fires of hell and her skin was still aglow with magic, but her expression and tone softened when she addressed me again, "You must not call upon anyone else, if you want the gift of prophecy to save your people."

I clasped my hands together behind my back. I would sell my soul to Satan himself to save my siblings, my friends, and my village. I think I had.

"Inhale" the witch commanded, bringing a cup of odorous vapors to my face.

I did as she asked.

"Touch the stone," she ordered.

I needed her to guide me there. My vision had blurred, and my steps faltered. I put my hands on the obsidian column, expecting it to be cool. To my surprise, the stone was hot to the touch. I squeezed shut my faltering eyes. As the pillar consumed me, I had one thought. Let me be an oracle or let me burn.

I burned.

CHAPTER
TWENTY-FIVE

The walls shuddered with my scream. Light flashed from my outstretched arm, burning a hole through a flatscreen and the tapestry hanging behind it. The flash left a scorch mark on the wall.

Suddenly Hermes was in my line of vision. He snaked an arm around me, pulling my body against his. His voice was warm and soothing as he said, "It's alright, Lydia. I'm here. You're safe with me."

It took few more panicked breaths to realize I was in a hotel room bed with Hermes, not burning to death via cursed column. It took even longer before I found words.

"Nightmare?"

I shook my head. "I think it's more than that. I'm having vivid hallucinations of what I think is the past while I make predictions."

"Are you saying you can see the tapestry woven while reading the strands of the next weave?" Hermes asked without missing a beat, in the same tone you used if you asked if someone liked cream in their coffee. His hand stroked my hair and back. His gaze was intent on my face, not the damage I'd caused. That was something he obviously didn't deem to be as important as my nightmares.

"Yes. I think so." I bit my lip, forming my thoughts into a coherent explanation. "I thought I was dreaming, but the visions are all connected. I take the perspective of women, who I think might be my ancestors. The last was from Arachova. No matter what transpires, Dione is a central figure."

He mulled this over for a second, his hand sliding down the length of my spine and resting on my lower back. I liked the weight of it there, steadying me while I waded through murky thoughts.

"Describe what you can remember."

As I described the visions as best as I could, I watched his face, finding no judgment **there**. He listened as if every word I had to say was the most important thing he ever heard.

"Dione was on the side of the Olympians when they dethroned Cronus and his supporters," he said after I finished. "That's why she's not in Tartarus. Are you sure it was her that you saw, or perhaps you're mistaken, and you saw someone who resembled her?"

"Except, during the last vision, they all knew she was Dione."

"You witnessed the origins of your family line, one of the battles of the Titanomachy, and something that might explain why many potential oracles died during the Turkish invasion of Greece. We'd thought it was the human invaders, but that pillar sounds like the gate to Tartarus. It would kill any mortal who touched it."

"The gate to Tartarus is where Jen and Brad were taking me!"

Hermes angled his head, confusion limning his handsome face. "Who is this Jenanbrad?"

"Jen *and* Brad. Like Jennifer Anniston and Brad Pitt?" I chuckled at his continued confusion, patting his bare chest. We'd have time to talk hot couples of the past later.

His gaze dipped to my hand.

I withdrew it. "Jen and Brad is what I call Echidna and Typhon. Makes them less scary."

A smile graced his pretty mouth. "Ah, it is comforting when you refer to the Titans, who frighten you, as familiar figures from your culture. I will remember this in the future. I don't wish for you to be scared." He squeezed me and nodded to the wall. Mirth danced in his eyes. "It's too dangerous."

I shuddered.

"Is Arachne going to be angry?"

She was frightening enough without the added element of being pissed off because I damaged her television.

"No. I will compensate her for the damages. ——-Which is Jen and which is Brad?"

I explained which is which and why.

After I finished, he said, "This is worrisome."

"It is? I can call them by their names, if it bothers you." So much for thinking of my comfort.

He waved his hand as if dismissing the thought. "No. Dione was in all of your visions, but it was Jen and Brad who kidnapped you. However, they are Dione's kin. The three might be working together." He squeezed me tight, and I don't think on purpose, as he added, "Three Titans is a lot to go up against. You'll need me and Spot. Perhaps I can get Arachne to leave her post here."

I shuddered at the notion. "I—I have a phobia of spiders."

"She's a person, Lydia, not a spider. Well, not completely a spider. She is their mother."

"That's worse," I whispered.

He stroked my hair. "Let Arachne feel useful. She's been banned from Olympus for so long. It might do her some good to be around her kind for a while."

"Banned from Olympus? I thought she was from Earth."

He shook his head. "No, she's from our world, not this one. Legends are sometimes borne of stories of men, not the truth."

It didn't escape my notice that he'd said, "our world". I wasn't from Olympus. Something occurred to me though. "If all the visions were perspectives from my ancestors, does that mean I'm Dione's descendent?"

"All oracles are."

I rubbed the bridge of my nose. That meant I was part Titan, very, very, *very* fractionally, but still. Perhaps that explained the literally explosive fear earlier.

"Alright, if Arachne wants to come with us, sure."

Hermes kissed the top of my head, then my lips. Our second kiss was as dreamy as the first. A little more so because the length of his hard body was pressed against my soft flesh.

Unfortunately, Cerberus decided to bark his heads off, reminding me I had a guard dog to let out of the car.

WHILE I LET Cerberus hunt in the prairie behind the hotel, Hermes negotiated with Arachne. A few hours later, I had a god and two monsters in the rental heading to Washington. I couldn't be happier. The trio made great company.

Arachne was an excellent conversationalist with plenty of stories. Turned out, Arachne's hotel had been for supernaturals.

"Pre-unveiling, Bigfoots, hobgoblins, halflings who look a little less like a mundane and a lot more like their fae parents, nephil who wanted to spread their wings while on the road, cryptids, shifters, and other non-human looking supes all stopped by to be who they were," Arachne said, her knitting needles clicking away in the rear.

"How did you avoid mundanes trying to stay there?" It was weird to call humans anything other than humans—let alone talk to spider-person from another world. However, I quickly caught on that supernaturals who had humanish looks didn't like to say human. They liked to say mundane and supernaturals and left the humanity out of it. Maybe saying mundane versus supernatural, or "supe," made them feel less like monsters and more like those with magic and those without.

"I got a witch to set up wards around the perimeter to dissuade mundanes." Her knitting needles didn't stop clicking as she spoke.

I pulled onto the highway. Traffic seemed heavier than most of our trip. "How'd did that work?"

In my rearview mirror, Arachne shrugged her thin shoulders. Her eyes were on her work: the same afghan-in-progress from last night. "The witch said they'd feel unease or foreboding. No one wants to sleep somewhere they think something bad will happen to them."

"Interesting that she could target the spell specifically for mundanes," Hermes said, rubbing his chin.

A yummy five o'clock shadow started there, which gave his pretty face a more rugged look. Even his slightly tousled curls looked good that way. He also manifested casual clothes that matched the look of the area: jeans, tank and a flannel. Very Greek god cowboy chic.

Sigh. My messy bun, emphasis on the messy, hoodie, and leggings didn't begin to match up.

Arachne chuckled, bringing my attention back to her. "Oh, Ezmal and her sisters have been at it for a long, long time."

Hermes reared his head and then turned halfway in his seat to look at Arachne fully. "Ezmal? The *Ezmal*?"

"Didn't know there was more than one."

I had no idea why this witch was a big deal.

Hermes didn't relent. "The Baba Yaga coven created the World Destroyer spell. I thought you'd changed. Now you tell me that you not only gave those evil women refuge but let them perform their magic on your land."

Baba Yaga. Now that was a name that even *I* had heard of. Luke had a book of world fairytales I used to read him when he was sick of Greek legends. In the book, the Baba Yaga was a singular witch in the woods from Slavic folklore. Sometimes good. Sometimes evil.

"I host a lot of supes without judging their past," the elderly woman sniffed. "They took very little in the way of payment for their services. They live in this world approved by the authorities."

Hermes turned around, jaw tightening. He seemed unconvinced that the witches were anything but trouble.

"Have you met the Supernatural Council of the Americas?" I asked her, hoping to change the subject.

I could hear the smile in Arachne's voice as she replied, "Lucinda the siren is a friend of mine. She brings me yarn and Seattle coffee, and occasionally some wine from the Washington wineries. As for the rest of the council, I try to mind my business, so I don't have to see the archangel. Handsome as he is dangerous, that one. I think if he didn't have that halfling witch girlfriend, Miriam, he'd be a bad egg."

"How so?" Hermes asked.

Cerberus made one of his dreaming sounds. We all glanced at him.

Arachne paused her knitting to scratch the sleeping fake black lab behind the ears. "Ezmal says he means well, very protective of his people and a fair leader. However, he likes running things too much. Power could get to his head. Gabriel needs a mate more powerful than he is to keep him balanced."

Hermes stroked his chin. "How is a halfling more powerful than a nephil? He's the son of the angel Gabriel."

The rhythmic click of her needles resumed. "She's the Mórrígan or at least one aspect of the goddess. Her daughter and another witch halfling are the other two."

Hermes nodded, face grim. "I'd heard. Wanted to know if you'd heard the same."

"I met the whole council," I offered for Arachne's benefit. "Didn't get to know much about them. I spent most of the time with a fae prince named Phyr while they debated about what to do with me."

"Lucky you!" Arachne exclaimed. "He's a charmer, that fae. Made this old lady blush."

Hermes snorted. "He'd make you blush until he sucked every last drop of your ichor as he boiled your bones in a fae stew." He gave me a serious look. "Never trust a fae. They gain power by eating the powerful."

I shuddered. Phyr had been inside my head.

"Vicious lies," Arachne spat, her needles stopped clicking. "Next, you'll say that I devour children."

"No, only men who harm their women," Hermes replied with no trace of amusement.

I glanced in my rearview to see her reaction. Arachne shrugged and began knitting, not denying his accusation.

"Works for Deer Lady. Why not me?"

Okaaaay. Arachne wasn't completely the sweet old lady. The monster had fangs.

Hermes shook his head. "Athena will never forgive you if you don't stop."

Now I was really confused. In my grandparents' story, Arachne was the one who was abused by Athena. I noted to ask him for the story later outside of her company. I couldn't ask her. By the way Arachne glared daggers at the back of the god's head, Hermes had broached a touchy subject.

"Athena will realize one day that there was nothing to forgive," Arachne replied, needles clicking again. "That gorgon was no good and would've led Athena down the same path. Her flesh was as corrupted as her ways."

Hermes grunted. "You should've let Athena learn on her own. In case you haven't heard, she's the Goddess of Wisdom."

"We're all unwise when it comes to first loves," Arachne replied with a heavy sigh.

The god and monster exchanged a rueful look.

"I brought up old wounds," Hermes said. "I apologize. I know firsthand what it is to have my feelings unrequited."

Except for the sounds of clicking needles and Cerberus's snore, the car fell silent. A tear slid down my cheek over my own first love.

TWENTY-SIX

We reached Eastern Washington by late afternoon. I had my mother's address in the GPS of the rental, but it didn't look right.

The four of us were at a rest stop near Yakima. We'd eaten some gas station food a couple hours ago that didn't want to stay put for me or Arachne, and Cerberus needed to run.

I left the elderly woman to take care of business in the big stall and had rejoined Hermes who was playing with Cerberus in a picnic area. Hermes threw a bone the length of my arm. I had no idea where he got the bone or what kind of animal it came from.

"Why does the address exist, but I can't see the town of Milagro Bay on the GPS. Is her shop in the country?" I asked Hermes, watching the pooch chase the long throw. I didn't like the idea of the isolation of the country.

The god chuckled and shook his curly head. "Milagro Bay is a village, not pasture, but it isn't on any map."

"The address is on a map."

"For your eyes. No mundane would ever perceive it."

Cerberus caught the bone midair, much higher than an ordinary dog should. No one milling about seemed to notice the giant bone or the extraordinary leap.

I posted my hands on my hips and turned to Hermes. "My map is digital. How does that work?"

"Magic." The god gestured to the dog who wasn't a dog. "Camouflage and illusions."

In other words, the information is above my pay grade. I got it. There were things even in the mundane world that I didn't know how they worked but used them every day. I couldn't for the life of me say how an airplane worked, but I knew there were engineers who did. Company secrets.

As if reading my face, Hermes replied, "Some have a deeper understanding of magic than others. I don't know why you can see it on your map, but I know there's spellwork behind it. I also know that no mundane could step foot in Milagro Bay unless a supernatural invited them. Our priestesses and oracles have always set temples in places where there are ley lines, as is your mother's property on Milagro Bay. Ley lines are magical connections between universes, and towns set there are hubs. The universe in which you live is one of many. "

"So, gods and supernaturals are aliens?"

The corner of his mouth twitched. "Yes, to the people of this world. To us, they're the aliens."

There he went, including me in an 'us' statement. "The conspiracy theorists would have a field day with this knowledge." Something else occurred to me. "Wait. If Olympus and Hades are simply worlds in different universes, how can the dead go to Hades?"

"The concept of an afterlife was formed by mortals because we shared the knowledge of the concept of ascension. The mundane belief is that the core conscience of a person or a soul can continue to exist. They believed it so strongly that it came to fruition." He smiled. "King Aidoneus was furious that his refuge from Olympus was invaded with shades. Persephone is a much better shepherd of these so-called souls."

I rubbed my temples, trying to grasp what he just divulged. "You're saying that belief in the afterlife made an afterlife possible?"

"Yes. Human belief is a magic in itself. That is why the angels covet devotion to their creator. It gives them more power by association. Their creator already ascended into a formless entity beyond comprehension." He blew out his breath and ran a hand over his mussed curls. "Even his own. The price of ascension is that you don't keep who you are. You have no will of your own, but unimaginable power."

I snorted. "What's the use of unimaginable power if you can't use it?"

"Now you know why some of us choose to not ascend." He flashed straight white teeth. The smile illuminated his handsome face. "Flesh has its perks."

I touched my lips. It certainly did.

"You two about ready?"

Not hearing Arachne's approach, I jumped.

The old spider-woman cackled. "Still got it." She squeezed my shoulder with a hand that appeared deceptively frail but had a vice-like grip. "Don't worry. I'm not a threat to you. You're a good person. Deep down. Deep, deep, deep, down."

I gazed into her watery brown eyes, magnified by the thick cat-eyeglasses. Mischief sparked in the depths. Managing a smile, I replied, "Thanks."

"Ooh, the sarcasm is thick! I like it. If I were a few thousand years younger, I'd court you." She let go, her gaze sweeping to Hermes. "Must be nice to look young forever."

"It is," Hermes replied through his teeth. It was then I noticed his hand lifting from the dagger at his belt, as he relaxed.

～

With many pitstops for my travel crew of four, it took well into the night to reach Clallam in Western Washington. You learn a lot of things about people, after seventeen hours stuck in a car together.

Hermes liked pop music with fast tempos. He'd drum out the beats on the dashboard and quickly learned the lyrics. The god had a great singing voice.

I could do without the drumming.

Arachne liked the window cracked and to hum to herself, off key. She'd click her needles and bring up a story that a song would remind her of. Arachne enjoyed gas station hotdogs as much as Cerberus.

Cerberus farted in his sleep mysteriously more often than before Arachne joined us.

Despite the excessive flatulence, I liked having the three as companions. I'd be sad to see them leave.

As we pulled up to the sleepy town of Milagro Bay, set on the Strait of Juan de Fuca, there wasn't a traffic light, only four way stops with no signage. The main street possessed a row of houses and buildings that could be a movie set. Even in the dark, the words *"quaint"* and *"magical"*, in a way towns that were impossibly cute were magical, came to mind. Save a few houses with second floor lights blazing, most of the residences and all the businesses were dark.

Carlo hated this type of town, but I no longer had to run a con game. After the life I'd lived for almost thirty years, I could enjoy a place where they roll in the sidewalks at eight pm.

"The entire town is populated with supernaturals," Hermes explained. "Mundanes come in either invited, or as tourists looking for bigfoot, or to visit the National Park, but there's nowhere for them to live in Milagro Bay."

"Supernaturals of the Greek variety?" I asked. I almost said mythology, but since I'd been to Olympus and Hades, I couldn't very well call it a myth.

"Some. You'll be among cryptids of this world, and sea creatures who originated from many worlds but call this place home. Harpies nest here. They'll make themselves known to you."

My mother had been in love with a harpy. Would Nicky consider herself my stepmom and Luke's granny? I doubted it. I hoped my mother's former partner was at least pleasant. Harpies didn't exactly have the best reputation.

"Turn down this alley," Hermes directed to a narrow lane tucked between a Victorian house that reminded me of the Painted Ladies of San Francisco, and a four-story, brick and mortar building that looked like something out of the old west. I would've missed the turn if he hadn't pointed it out. GPS wasn't even working here, and my burner cell had no signal.

"The parking is in the rear."

Sure enough, behind the Victorian there was a gravel lot and a garage. A shadowy figure stood next to a sleek Bugatti Mistral parked in front of the garage. I wasn't a car person, but Carlo had always wanted a Bugatti.

I parked the rental car next to the luxury car, feeling a bit shabby and a lot curious.

"It's Dione," Hermes whispered. "She can find her blood anywhere."

Arachne snored peacefully, but Cerberus stirred.

"We're here," I said, hoping to wake my new monster friend without being obvious that I needed her.

The dream where the Greek village girl trusted Dione, ending in her demise was fresh in my mind. So was the fact that Dione took my mother twice. Once when I was a child, and the second when she tried to use her to unlock the gates of Tartarus.

Arachne roused, smacking her lips. "Something foul is afoot. The air don't taste right."

Cerberus sniffed the air. A low growl followed.

The Titan stepped into the light, revealing she was indeed Dione.

I opened the door to my car, ready to face my distant relative. Anger welled inside, hot and fierce. She killed my ancestor, and she likely killed my mother.

Hermes grimaced. "I don't think she's alone."

"What should we do?" I asked, voice cracking. One Titan was scary enough. Dione was older than Hermes or Arachne, she'd accumulated wealth here on this world. It's the first thing I noticed about her. Wealthy people had a lot of worship in this country, a form of idolatry that bordered religion.

None of which bode well for us.

"I could carry you off to Olympus right now," Hermes said.

I peered at Arachne and Cerberus in the rearview. I hadn't known either for long, but they were my friends, here to help me. Then I thought of my boy Luke. He had Dione's blood. I couldn't risk putting my friends and son in danger.

I was no innocent village girl. If I died, I'd have done plenty to deserve it. I could only hope that I'd preserve my memories so Persephone could tell the Olympians they had a traitor in their midst.

"No." I unbuckled my seatbelt. "I'm going to face her. We will get this over with one way or another."

I hoped Arachne, Hermes, and Cerberus would stay in the car, but there was no chance of that. Probably wouldn't matter anyway.

"Dione," I said, climbing out of the car. "Kinda not cute to make me come all this way just to kill me. Could've done it back east and spared me the lower back pain."

Hermes drew to my right and Arachne silently sidled to my left. Cerberus stalked from between us. The harmless, black Labrador façade exchanged for the three headed monster hound of Hades. His stance read that in no uncertain terms would the three Titans get past him.

"I'm not trying to kill you. I would never harm my kin."

"The memories that come to me in my dreams say otherwise."

"You can read threads of the weave of the past? Your gift

surpasses many generations of previous oracles." Dione took a step forward, a slight smile touching her painted lips.

Cerberus growled in warning.

I glanced at Hermes. He nodded. Dione was telling the truth.

Dione raised her hands. "Peace, Cerberus. I won't harm her. I only want to talk." To me, she said, "If you examine closely, you'll see that I've never harmed anyone."

"Maybe not directly, but I saw you lead an initiate oracle to the gate of Tartarus. She trusted you because she had no choice. She died trying to become an oracle. Echidna, your relative, was the last person my mother saw. Did you somehow convince my mom to the same fate," I replied, hoping the others would assume that I extracted the information from the weave. I've bluffed and lied by omission plenty of times, but this time it felt...wrong. Perhaps because I didn't want to lie to Hermes and Arachne. They'd done nothing but be kind to me. "Or did you ambush her like you did me?"

"As far as what you think you saw regarding your ancestor's death, it's not accurate. What happened to your mother was a tragic mistake. I'll explain, if you give me a chance." She dared another step.

All three of Cerberus's heads started barking. I soon discovered that it wasn't Dione my dog was warning to stay back.

A second figure appeared from the shadows and a third, massive figure appeared, filling the entire alley. Brad and Jen joined the welcoming party.

TWENTY-SEVEN

Typhon said something in a sonorous voice, but he spoke in ancient Greek, or a language close to it, so I could only pick up "kill."

Hermes responded in the same language. The two started shouting, but I couldn't understand or even hear enough over the increasingly frantic barking dog.

Thunder added to the noise. A lightning bolt shot from Typhon's fingers, striking Hermes. The god stumbled backward, crashing to the ground.

Someone screamed.

It was me, I realized.

I rushed to Hermes.

Cerberus, now the full three-headed vicious monster, attacked Dione. The Titan fought back.

I couldn't do anything about it. I didn't know how to control my lightning. Rain drenched my back as I crouched to check the god, with whom I hoped to have something special someday. Hope. That's all I had right now. If it was good enough for Pandora, it was good enough for me.

Arachne and Echidna fought somewhere nearby. Snakes and—*oh gods!*—an army of bowling ball-sized spiders swarmed the ground. Nightmare fuel for the rest of my life.

If I lived past this night.

Something clutched my hoodie, pulling me up. Typhon had been terrifying at a distance, looking at him from the windshield of my car. Up close and personal in his monstrous clutches, I could see the details of how hideous his form truly was. There was nowhere to rest my gaze that didn't horrify or nauseate me. The snakes slithering in and out of disgusting flesh; the heads making animal noises; the creepy creatures of unknown names crawling from his arm onto me. All of it was too much for my mind to comprehend and stay coherent.

Darkness rimmed my vision. I saw Echidna brawling with Arachne. Cerberus yelped as Dione struck the dog with an unseen force.

No!

I wouldn't pass out. I raged against it. I wouldn't die like this, and I certainly wouldn't let my friends die like this. I kicked, clawed, and finally screamed my rage.

A lightning bolt would sure be nice right now.

My scream seemed to be the most effective weapon.

Typhon swayed as if punched in all his heads.

He shouted something, shaking me like Cerberus shook his bones.

Pain shot through my back and again my vision dimmed.

No!

Recovering from the shake, I boiled over with fury. I should be at home, watching some baking competition on television with my husband. But, no, Carlo had to be a lying, cheating snake in the grass, and I had to be a freakin' oracle.

Below, Hermes pushed to his feet, his hand going to his dagger.

Typhon didn't notice, not yet anyway.

I screeched, pouring all my anger, all my frustration into it to distract him. It came out birdlike, like a falcon. But the sound was shriller, piercing as a needle.

Typhon's many heads roared and growled, hissing in pain.

Clouds roiled above. Lightning struck below.

Typhon shook me.

I screeched again, louder and angrier. As the Titan's grip released and I plummeted, my stomach hurtled into my throat.

To my surprise, I was caught again. A cacophony of falcon-like screeches answered my cry. Something dragged me upward, higher and higher. Out of Typhon's reach.

Dizzy from the drop and sudden lift, it took me a moment to register the flock of golden-feathered humanoid bodies and wings. Harpies, too numerous to count, bombarded the three Titans.

From my aerial view, I watched Jen stop fighting Arachne. She disappeared, snakes and all, vanishing before my eyes.

Storms clouds formed around Typhon like a mini tornado. The giant Titan vanished in the gathering cyclone. The tornado fizzled and died, nothing left in its place.

Dione wasn't so lucky. Harpies had the Titan hog-tied and were flying off. They too disappeared.

The harpy carrying me lowered me to the ground. Cerberus, uninjured, bounded to me. The harpies gave the hound from Hades a wide berth, so I got the full impact of his love. The big lug knocked me to the ground. All three heads took turns sniffing and licking me.

"You must really love hot dogs, Spot," I said, laughing a little too hard. My body trembled, the adrenaline still pumping through my veins.

Arachne approached, spiders climbing up her spindly legs and disappearing under her muumuu.

I could have gone an entire lifetime without seeing that.

What concerned me more than the spiders was that she appeared tired, and bled inky blood in places.

"Don't fret, kid. I'm not grievously wounded."

I spared her a small smile of gratitude. Then I glanced around the gathering harpies, seeking Hermes.

The flock parted to let the god through.

Hermes was as bad as Cerberus, embracing me in a tight squeeze before looking me over.

"Need a sniff?" I asked.

His brow furrowed in confusion. "A what?"

I shook my head. "Kidding."

He glanced at Cerberus and grinned. Relief washed over his features as his gaze returned to me. "Are you hurt?"

"Not anything permanent."

One of the harpies stepped forward. "That's good to hear."

I think she was the one who had plucked me from the air. Like the rest, she appeared human with birdish features: big, wide-set eyes, beak-like nose, sharp jaw and cheekbones, all on a narrow face.

"Thanks for the catch." I nodded to her. "I'm Lydia. The new Oracle to the gods."

A smile touched her human mouth. "Well, what do you know? Apollonia's girl is a harpy queen."

I blinked. "What?"

Arachne and Hermes exchanged a confused glance.

"You called us," another harpy answered. "We had to come."

I rubbed my temples. It wasn't enough to be part Titan of Dione's line of oracles, no, I had to be part harpy, and not just any harpy, a *queen*—whatever that meant. The notion of a monarch in this day and age was ridiculous.

"I'm Nicky, queen of the northwest harpies," said the one who'd spoken first. She offered her hand, her gaze taking me in. Her smile was warm and sweet, if not a bit nervous.

I took her hand tentatively. My own eyes welled up with tears as the old wound seared open my sternum. I was looking at the woman who would have been my stepmother. She might have raised me, if things weren't so messed up.

"Thank you, Nicky," I managed.

She swallowed hard, large eyes brimming with tears. "Even if you weren't a harpy queen, I'd come to help you. You see. I was your mother's life partner. I—I'm so happy to meet you, Lydia."

I nodded, embracing the harpy.

Nicky stiffened at first. Then wrapped me in her arms, folding golden wings around me.

"Oh, child," she whispered. "I've wanted to meet you for so long. I hope to be more than an occasional visitor and advisor. I've watched you grow up and loved you from afar your whole life."

Something in me broke, releasing forty years of hurt from my chest in the form great big sobs. I had a mother waiting for me this whole time. It might not have been the one who gave birth to me, but Nicky was my long-lost mother.

After I'd cried it all out with Nicky comforting me, we broke our embrace. I felt a little embarrassed because Hermes, Cerberus, Arachne and the harpies watched the whole thing unfold. Nobody but the dog had dry eyes.

Arachne blew her nose in a knitted length of material, making a honking sound. Hermes cut her a glare.

"What?" The elderly woman scoffed. "Like you weren't moved by the beauty and tragedy of it all."

TWENTY-EIGHT

Nicky cleared her throat and then addressed the harpies, "Patrol the town. Make sure the Titans aren't lurking and waiting for another opportunity to strike."

The harpies flew in sets of four. I wondered if they had formal teams or units like a military. They were Hades' army. Persephone's sirens were her army and seemed to fight in units when they took on the Titans. Growing up bombarded with patriarchal notions of masculinity and femininity, the all-girl armies were kind of cool.

Nicky slipped her arm around mine. "You must be tired. Why don't I show you your new home?"

"What did they do with Dione?"

"She's being taken to Olympus where she'll be tried. I suspected her part in your mother's murder. Her presence here with the Titans proved she had something to do with it."

Hermes touched my free arm. "I should go. Olympus will need my report to condemn her."

A lump formed in my throat as I turned away from Nicky to face him. I thought I'd gained everything. A mom, a wacky grand-mother, a dog, and a new man. Except Hermes wasn't a man. He was a god. A god with more duties than simply guarding me. Many he'd performed long before I was born, almost as long as my line existed.

"I guess it's goodbye then." I forced a smile. A new wound ripped open in my chest. Everyone left me, eventually. Why not him? Who was I to Hermes, anyway? I knew the stories. Gods fell for mortal women all the time, but not forever. I looked down at my hands, because looking into his face and not seeing what I'd seen before would hurt too much. "Thanks for your help getting me here. Take care."

Hermes hooked a finger under my chin, forcing me look into his dark eyes. "Not goodbye. I'll be back after I discuss a leave of absence with my father. That is, if you want me here."

Of course I did. I had a lot to learn, and I also wanted to see where this thing brewing between us was headed.

"I do."

His responding grin lit up his entire face.

"Good."

He leaned down, kissing me tenderly.

My toes curled in my shoes.

Cerberus nudged his head between us, breaking the kiss and our embrace apart. A black lab peered at us with puppy dog eyes.

"It's a good thing you're cute," I said.

Hermes laughed. One more quick peck on the cheek and he ran preternaturally fast, disappearing into the ether.

AFTER RETRIEVING MY SUITCASES, I followed Nicky onto a porch which wrapped around the entire house. Plants hung from the rafters, and planters of flowers lined the railing. There were two rocking chairs on the back with a table in between, and I'd seen a two-seater swing on the front. I got a good view of the exterior, albeit in short glimpses in the dark, when I'd turned off the street.

Also, when Typhon was swinging me around in the sky, he gave me a great aerial view.

Beyond the back door, was a mudroom. It had the appearance of being well-lived in but clean. A worn mat still had women's shoes about my size and some a size larger.

"I got most of my things moved out, but I guess I forgot those." Nicky gestured to the bigger shoes. "We used to take off our shoes because it gets pretty muddy around here and we didn't want to track, but you do as you please."

Not quite feeling like this place belonged to me yet, I took off my shoes.

"Here. You don't want your feet getting cold." Nicky handed me house slippers. "You're about the same size as Apollonia."

I slid my feet into my mother's slippers. The only thing of the small woman that would fit me. They were comfy.

"I don't wear the things," Arachne provided, wiping her eight legs on the mat outside the backdoor.

Nicky flipped on the lights for the kitchen. It was a chef's kitchen with marble counters, a gas stove, modern fridge, and an island with a sink and stools. Copper pots and cast-iron pans dangled from a four-sided rack above the island. Herbs hung to dry, making the place smell domestic, like a home. I would've loved a kitchen like this when Luke was small. This was a kitchen for a family.

"Nice kitchen," Arachne observed, doing a little side to side shuffle. "I need the powder room."

The harpy pointed to an ajar door next to the kitchen. "Should be clean and have what you need. If not, holler. I'll hear you."

After Arachne closed the door behind her, Nicky turned to me. "The pantry is fully stocked. I cleaned out the old food and some of my stuff I'd like to keep."

I squeezed her hand. "I'm sorry you had to leave your home."

Nicky waved it off. "Don't be. I moved out immediately after her funeral." Her eyes teared. "This place has too many memories. I'd rather move on."

"She's in Asphodel. Persephone keeps her there."

The harpy smiled ruefully and squeezed my shoulder. "I know. I just—" She shook her head. "Shades aren't really our dead loved ones but echoes. It's like talking to a hologram programmed with her memories, stiff and robotic. Apollonia was affectionate and sweet. I'm sorry that you had to interact with what was left."

I bit my lip and nodded. Saying any more would make me cry. In a way, I felt relieved. I didn't want that to be who my mother really was.

"You didn't share with Hermes that she was there?"

I shook my head.

"Good. He has to tell his father everything."

Arachne rejoined us as Nicky walked us through a hallway with wood flooring and walls that obviously lacked a few pictures. The rest were pictures of my grandparents, my mother as a youth, me from a young age until very recently. Some were with Carlo, and some were with Luke. Some were Luke as he looked now. My stomach knotted. I didn't recognize any of them as photos anyone I knew had taken, and they seemed to be snapped while we were out and about, doing things.

I shuddered. "Did my mother pay someone to take these?"

"Yes. I know it's probably disturbing, but it's how she stayed close without endangering you or your family. That and Hermes's reports," Nicky tossed over her shoulder.

It was weird to know my romantic interest had spied on me. It also made it weirder that he was interested in me.

"Hermes isn't a stalker. He had to watch you in order to protect you. You were the next Oracle," Nicky said, as if reading my mind.

Arachne snorted. "Still a bit creepy to be kissing on her at his age."

"I'm not exactly a spring chicken," I said, chuckling at the older woman.

"Yeah," Nicky agreed a little too readily. "Once a person reaches a certain maturity, age doesn't matter. Apollonia was about five hundred years younger than I am, more or less."

It took me a moment to process five hundred years younger. Just exactly how old was the harpy. Now that we were in good light, Nicky looked to be in her late thirties at most.

We passed through a cozy living space, with a brocade sofa and matching love seat, a recliner, and a wingback accent chair. Framed school pictures of Luke sat on a mantle above the fireplace, and a bureau had lots of old framed pictures of people I didn't know. Really old. Some were black and white. Some were painted portraits. But I saw the resemblance to me and my family, even Dione in a few.

My chest tightened. Dione was the only living family I had besides Luke.

Nicky kept moving to the stairs. She pointed to a door. "That's the consultation room and altar. Apollonia did most of her predictions there. It took a lot out of her and traveling to the temple in the mountains wasn't an ideal commute for Apollonia or the Neo-Greco pagans."

"Neo-Greco pagans?" I asked. "Never heard of the term."

Nicky looked at me, concern in her eyes. "You are the priestess who will lead the ceremonies."

Hermes had said something about that.

"Don't worry," Nicky said. "There is a guidebook that will help you. Plus, your mother had certain ceremonies recorded. I'll email them to you."

Not knowing what to say or how to feel about being a religious leader, I nodded.

"I was a priestess, long, long ago," Arachne offered, her voice soft and a touch fragile. "I don't know about neo doings, but I know the old ways."

I smiled, grateful that I had relented and let Hermes ask her to come. "Thank you."

We followed Nicky up the stairs which led to another hall. The walls were bare, but lighter spots evidenced there was art or pictures there before. A piece of me ached for Nicky. She'd lost a wife. A chapter of her life had closed, and she'd only had a matter of days to move out while grieving.

The harpy opened a door to a room with a heavy sigh. Without looking inside, she said, "There's a private bathroom attached to the suite. You go on, make yourself comfortable and get some sleep. I'll show Arachne to her room. We'll talk more in the morning."

I rolled my suitcases into my new room. Cerberus followed me in, circling on a throw rug between the foot of a four-poster bed and a large bureau. The hound of Hades shed his lab guise, settling all three heads on his paws and closing all six eyes.

"Guess you're sticking around for good."

The thought warmed me. I'd grown to care for the monster dog and his weirdo quirks.

The door shut behind me with a gentle click. The shuffle of footsteps and muffled voices followed, disappearing down the hall of the big old Victorian.

TWENTY-NINE

After a long, luxurious bubble bath and dressing, I placed the suitcase that contained my grandparents' belongings on my bed and opened it.

A very old skin with a lion's head lay on top. It had been on the wall of their home above the fireplace my whole life. I'd always hated it. A dead animal on the wall was pretty embarrassing, especially since lions native to Greece went extinct a long time ago. My grandfather once said that it was the Nemean Lion skin worn by Hercules, and then he told me the story of how the demigod killed it. I thought he was pulling my leg, but he had been so fond of the skin, I couldn't bear to get rid of the thing.

I carefully took the lion head and skin and laid it in the top drawer of the dresser until I could get something to hang it.

The next item was a hollow and twisted goat's horn. It had been on a shelf in my grandmother's kitchen. She said we'd never go hungry as long as we had the horn. I held it. Over the years, I'd struggled at times but always had enough to eat. Was she superstitious or was I holding the cornucopia?

Cerberus stirred, well, one head anyway. He eyed me for a

moment, sniffed the air and then went back to sleep as if all was right. I set the horn on an empty shelf on the wall. Best to keep these things in my room for now.

The next object to come out was ancient shearing scissors, said to be from a far distant ancestor who used them to shear Jason's golden fleece. The legend held so long in my family that the shears were passed down from generation to generation to shear the flocks. Then it was retired and kept as a good luck charm during shearing season. It had rested in the room where my grandmother kept her loom and the wool that she would buy occasionally, to weave a blanket or rug to give as gifts. Everyone loved my grandmother's finished weavings, but she refused to do it for profit.

"I'd die at the loom, burdened, instead of enjoying my gift."

The next item was another object from my grandmother's weaving room. A long, pale-yellow skirt made from tufts of different cuts of wool, some short and some long hairs. It was a perfect circle despite the mismatched material. However, the old fleece was worn and ugly, and didn't smell awesome up close, but it had been passed down like the shearing scissors. A treasured piece of my family's history.

I set the folded skirt in the same drawer as the lion skin.

The last item was a knife that also sat in their kitchen but was never used. It was old and had a beautiful, albeit worn, sheath. Knife was a stingy word for a blade so long that it needed a scabbard the length my forearm. However, my grandmother always called it a knife, so I followed suit.

The knife went under my pillow. It hadn't been taken out of its sheath my entire life, but I could put it to good use if need be. I wasn't going to be taken without anything to defend myself again.

I climbed into a bed that smelled of my grandmother's house, hitting me with nostalgia. The blanket was something she'd woven; I was sure of it. In a torrent of memories, a fuzzy picture of the blanket on my mother's bed in our small apartment surfaced.

My mom slept here and lived a whole life I knew nothing about.

She was someone to many people, a priestess and an oracle. Sharp teeth tore through my chest, gnawing at the wound. That wound had existed there for too much of my life. I wiped my eyes with the back of my hands.

I would never get my mother back, nor anything that might have been different. I only had right now.

I got a burner phone from one of my bags and called Luke's cell. I had the number memorized. When you have a husband like Carlo, it was always the 1980s. I had all the important numbers memorized. So, when I got no answer from Luke, I tried his landline.

"Hello. This is Juan speaking." He sounded pretty tired, but there was also a tension in his voice.

"Heya, Juan. Luke around?" I was careful not to identify myself.

"Uh—" Rustling and movement in the background preceded a door closing. He asked in a low voice, "Where are you, ma? Uh. Wait. Never mind. Don't want to know. Are you safe?"

"I'm safe." *As I can be.*

"You might want to lay low for a bit. The feds took Luke for questioning a day ago. Said he wasn't under arrest, but I haven't heard from him since."

I sat up straighter. "Luke's in jail? He didn't do anything wrong."

"I don't know. His cell is dead. I've got a lawyer working on it. He was taken by a special international agency. ISEA? I've never heard of it. They run within their own framework like Interpol, apparently. I don't get it. Luke isn't a supernatural."

My gut churned. I'd never heard of it either. "What does ISEA stand for?"

There was some background noise. "It says on the card the agent gave me that she was from the International Supernatural Enforcement Agency."

I'd never heard of it, making me worry it was made up.

"I'll see what I can do, Juan. I have some connections who might be able to help. You hold tight, okay?"

"I'll try. I'm scared."

"I am too, but we'll get through this. Luke and I are innocent. We had nothing to do with his father's crimes. They can't keep him forever."

"I'm glad you called. Love you, ma."

"Me too, Juan. Love you, too."

CHAPTER

THIRTY

Right after I hung up, I went downstairs. There was no way I was going to sleep with Luke missing. I didn't buy this ISEA nonsense. It was likely something else. Probably Thetis and whoever she was colluding with.

Nicky was in the kitchen, mixing something in a bowl. From a glance at the ingredients on the counter—milk, flour, sugar, baking powder, blueberries, and eggs, to name a few—she was in the middle of making blueberry muffins. "I thought I'd have some breakfast ready for the two of you. Need something before bed?"

"Luke was taken by ISEA agents for questioning. His father is a criminal, so his fiancé assumed it was about that."

She stopped stirring. "ISEA agents don't care about mundane crimes. They police *us*."

"I don't think Luke committed a supernatural crime. My very recently ex-husband is at large."

"Sounds like this is going to take a while." She pointed to the table with her lips. "Have a seat, I'll get this batter poured out and brew some coffee."

"I can do the latter."

She directed me to the coffee grounds and maker.

While I got the coffee started and she poured the muffins, I explained everything about Carlo's exploits and crew, Luke's move out west, and what Juan had just told me.

I poured the coffee into two mugs from the cupboard above the coffee maker.

Nicky put the muffin pans in the oven and set a timer. "The ISEA arrest could be unrelated, or Luke could have any number of latent magics from your side of the family. ISEA knows of your existence. Your mother registered your magic with an archangel. The angels work with ISEA because the organization worked to their benefit before supes revealed themselves. Witch trials, monster hunters, all that was part of ISEA's past. They even used to be called United Nations Monster Unit."

She poured cream from a little pitcher and doled out sugar cubes from a real sugar cube jar, handing me a tiny spoon.

The little touches reminded me of my grandmother. Nicky felt like family and though her news frightened me, I felt safer having someone knowledgeable on my side. Something occurred to me.

"I met the Archangel of the Americas and the supernatural council. Aren't they based in Washington?"

"The Seattle Eastside suburbs. About a two-hour drive from here depending on traffic. I think they would be your best bet. Contacting them would be a better choice than going directly to ISEA. They might want to question you."

"Do you know how to contact them?"

"I do." She grinned over her coffee cup. "The numbers for the office of the archangel and the Supernatural Council of the Americas are on their website. But it's not office hours for either. You'll have to call in the morning."

THE NEXT MORNING, I was up with the sun. Nicky was already downstairs having breakfast with Arachne.

I let Cerberus, who had slept in my room, out back with a warning, "Don't go beyond the property and don't kill any cats or dogs, Spot."

The hound glanced over his shoulder, preternatural intelligence in his soft brown eyes. He woofed and went on his way.

Cerberus might have looked like a black lab, but he wasn't a mundane dog. I wasn't going to insult him with a leash. Since this was a supernatural town, I doubted anyone would be afraid of him or report a loose dog wandering my lot.

Nicky slapped a sticky note on the table. On it was a phone number written in neat script. "Office of the Archangel is your best bet. Gabriel Crowfoot is a liaison for ISEA. He doesn't take kindly to any supe being mistreated by mundane authorities or anyone."

I swallowed. "He also doesn't like me very much."

Over breakfast I explained what had happened at the gates of Tartarus.

"Sounds like he was assessing whether you were a threat or an ally. You left his partner's faerie. You're good."

I called the number.

"You've reached the office of the Archangel Gabriel Crowfoot," a professional feminine voice answered.

"Hi, my name is Lydia. I recently met the archangel and the council and I need their help—what the..." I rose as I saw a flash in the yard through the kitchen window.

Three dogs barked. Cerberus, warning whomever off.

Nicky bolted out the back door.

I rose and followed, unsure of what I'd do to help, but I did have my grandmother's dagger at my hip.

Arachne got up slowly, parts cracking and popping. "Wish I could finish my coffee before trouble came knocking."

Cerberus trotted over to me and put himself bodily between me and the new arrivals. Fortunately, the people I needed to see were in the back lot. I recognized the council.

"Sorry to have scared your hound, Child of Olympus," Phyr said to me.

Gabriel had no wings this time, wore a t-shirt and *oh my* grey sweats. If he weren't so scowly, he'd be kinda gorgeous.

Miriam waved, looking less freaky than the first time I saw her, with her white antlers and strange skin and hair. Maybe because she was in leggings, a t-shirt for a bakery, and she had her hair pulled back in a bun.

Phyr smiled in my direction, bronze and beautiful as any god. He wore the same sort of t-shirt. Maybe the council members ran a bakery on the side?

The pretty, plus-sized gal named Leilani waved. Cian, her husband, stayed close by her side, nodding.

Instead of a bigfoot, there was a tall, willowy blonde, who I assumed was Aurora. She was a new-age vision in her broom skirt and tie-dye tank. Princess, a gorgeous biker girl, wrapped her arm around the tall woman's waist in a way that said they were definitely a couple.

The law enforcers Shawn and Micah weren't there, nor were the two twenty-somethings Jada and Roxy.

The siren Lucinda and Nicky locked gazes.

From my grandmother's legends, harpies were Hades' law enforcement and sirens were Persephone's army. They should be allies.

A smile broke out on each woman's face. Arachne waved at Lucinda and got an equally bright smile and wave back.

"We heard reports of a fight. What happened here?" Gabriel asked.

So much for office hours. Also, one or multiple neighbors were snitches for the council. I'd keep that in mind. In the meantime, I explained how Jen and Brad showed up with Dione.

Lucinda looked at Nicky. "Dione was the only one you managed to capture?"

"Yes. My squad took her to Olympus to be tried by the king and his Olympian family."

The shorter woman stepped forward. "You didn't think to notify me?"

Nicky's feathers ruffled. Literally. "I don't answer to the queen, and this is a matter between the Titans and the Olympians."

"A supe was murdered in our territory," Gabriel said. "It's our business. Your king signed a treaty."

"With the angels, not you."

I touched Nicky's arm.

"I was just on the phone with your receptionist, calling about the whole thing," I said, trying to diffuse the situation. The tension here was thick and it was only going to get thicker if I let them bicker about Dione's capture.

Gabriel pulled his phone from his sweats and made a call. He spoke to someone in what sounded like Portuguese then hung up. "It tracks."

Okay. There were some definite trust issues here. I'd have to win him over if I was going to see Luke again. "Why don't you all come in, have some of Nicky's muffins, and I can tell you about the other reason I called?"

"Will you need all of us?" Miriam asked, eyeing Cerberus. He was back from three head mode to one head mode. By the way she looked at the hound, I didn't think Miriam was a dog person. "Some of us need to go to work now that the reported threat is over."

"Depends. I need to talk to someone in the ISEA about why they took my son."

CHAPTER
THIRTY-ONE

The council left, except Gabriel, Lucinda, and Phyr. Why the fae prince remained, I didn't know. However, I suspected he was someone like Hermes, able to cross the multiverse easily.

Turned out, angel boy possessed a direct line to one of the top ISEA agents, Emily Tan. He paced the floor while Gabriel spoke to Agent Tan.

"Her son is a latent and lives on the west coast. He couldn't possibly be connected to his father's crimes, Agent Tan," he said, tone brokering no argument. After a brief pause, his expression shifted to cool neutrality. "Yes. That's a different story. Yes. That many people affected would be hard to contain."

My heart sank. Did Luke know his father was about to leave because he was a part of the scam? Was that why he'd called? Why would ISEA want him for that? Also, I couldn't imagine my sweet boy involved in crime. Luke had always been my boy scout. Why would the kid who didn't like lies involve himself in a scam?

"I see. It sounds like a case of latent abilities awakening, not fraud...uh huh...He has no priors and had no idea he had this ability

—okay. Okay. Abilities. If you put him in my custody for a probationary period, I'd consider it a personal favor." He smiled. The archangel was too handsome, too perfect when he smiled.

I'm sure he won lots of people over with his smile, but not me. That was the smile of someone powerful getting his way. At least he was using his position for my son, but I had a feeling if Gabriel Crowfoot called in a favor, you owed him.

"Yes. We have a deal. Always good to take someone off your case load and owe you in the process." He chuckled at his own joke, but there was no mirth in his eyes. The guy was good. Politicians usually were.

Nicky watched Gabriel, too. The harpy's expression gave away nothing. Not much emoting coming from anyone sitting around my kitchen. Arachne was knitting. Lucinda was on her phone, texting. Phyr scratched behind the erstwhile vicious guard monster's ears. Too bad, no one had an opinion.

I would love someone else's insight into this archangel. He must wield a lot of power in the supernatural world, if he can just call an international agency and be entrusted with the custody of a supernatural.

Phyr and I made eye contact. He smiled slightly.

I didn't trust Gabriel at first either. He is powerful and likes leading others, too much. In my experience, those types of leaders tend to abuse their authority and make life difficult for everyone under their so-called protection.

I glanced around to see if anyone else had heard the fae's voice.

I'm speaking telepathically and can read your thoughts. Stop looking directly at me so we can communicate freely. Also, stop making that face. It's concerning. You look like you're going to experience a seizure.

The last bit surprised me the most. I usually mastered my expressions so that clients wouldn't know how I really felt.

If he likes wielding authority so much, why do you trust him?

Because at the core, he does not change. There, I see a person who wants to do the right thing. A protector and guide, not an authoritarian.

He does know how to play the political game to look like, as Miriam puts it, an alphahole. It's an act. He takes the counsel of others and doesn't overstep his authority.

It took all my self-control not to laugh at the word alphahole.

He uses his position of power to help those who have none. That is a leader. As long as our interests align, I would follow Gabriel anywhere.

I couldn't help but hear a note of admiration in his tone...in my head. Also, I couldn't help but trust Phyr's admission that he has his own interests. I doubt he'd share them with me, but it was good to know.

Gabriel hung up. "Alright. The good news is I can get Luke out. The bad news is your boy is going to have to stay with you in Milagro Bay until he has his supernatural gifts under control. He can't go in oracle mode and make doomsday predictions in public like that again."

A smile spread on Nicky's face as a frown formed on mine. Luke had my same ability, and obvious lack of control of it, but he'd signed no contract. So many questions came to mind.

"How is he supposed to do that?"

Gabriel gave me a hard look. "I assume you and the harpies know more about that than I would."

I swallowed hard as I nodded. I didn't know how to use any of my so-called gifts, they worked however they felt like working and whenever. However, the harpies certainly knew their stuff.

What worried me was this new impediment to my son's freedom. Luke had a life, a career, and a fiancé. He wasn't going to like having to live with me here, and he definitely wasn't going to like it when I told him I didn't know how to use my gifts and couldn't help him. He already resented that I had refused to leave his father years ago. I feared I'd lose my son with him right there as a reminder that I'd failed. Again.

∾

WITHIN A COUPLE OF HOURS, Luke stepped out of a black vehicle in the lot of my new home. As soon as he was out, the vehicle sped off. I didn't get a good look at the driver, and they seemed to want nothing to do with us.

I didn't care. My boy was here.

However, my boy was a boy no more. He had Carlo's square jaw and my grandfather's symmetry of features. Permanently sun-kissed olive skin of his Greek and Italian heritage. Curling black hair, a little mussed, was even more gorgeous than I remembered. His dark, soulful eyes took in the house, Cerberus, the strangers, paused for a bit extra on Arachne, Nicky, and Phyr, and then his gaze landed on me.

Thick eyebrows pressed together in a scowl. Confusion limned his features. "Ma?"

My stomach knotted and I squeezed my hands together so he wouldn't see me tremble. My eyes, however, betrayed me. A single tear, hot and wet, escaped. Soon, others joined them.

"Hey there, Lukie."

I opened my arms, hoping for an embrace but fully expecting rejection via a wave or a nod of acknowledgement after so long.

My son walked into my arms, hugging me tightly.

"*You* got me out of that place, ma?"

I nodded and then looked at Gabriel standing next to me. "With the help of Mr. Crowfoot here."

Luke backed away from the hug and sized the older man up. They could be twins in build. Tall and muscular. The two of them were handsomer than movie stars.

"Thank you." Luke narrowed his eyes. "If I may ask, how do you know my mom and why are you doing her favors?"

There was a lot of accusation in his tone. Was he *protecting* me from a possible suitor?

Gabriel held up his hands. "I have no romantic intentions. I'm part of the Supernatural Council of the Americas. It's my job to see that the mundane authorities don't overstep mine." He was all the leader now. The arrogance of someone who was used to calling the shots and being obeyed laced his tone as he added, "You were released to my custody. I'm handing that custody over to your mother and will check in with you both on your progress through Lucinda here, since she is associated with your pantheon."

Lukie made a face at "your pantheon", but my smart boy said nothing. He learned from me and Carlo that it was better to listen up and get what someone wanted than to ask the wrong questions.

The siren raised her hand and waved, but she didn't look happy about it. Must be nice to just tell your co-council members what they had to do.

"When you're ready to return to the mundane world, you may. If you make all your check-ins, remain here in Milagro Bay, and show a proficiency with your magic, no charges will be pressed for the incident."

"Got it," Luke said. "What about my fiancé? Is he welcome here?"

"Of course," Nicky and I said at once.

The owner of the house and the protector of the town might have answered, but Luke's gaze was on Gabriel. When did my son stop looking to me for answers? I'd always been his shield when he was in school.

The archangel glanced at Nicky briefly before turning his attention back to my son. "Since the mayor is fine with a mundane in a supernatural town, so am I."

THIRTY-TWO

Phyr, Lucinda, and Gabriel left shortly after. It was then I explained our family story as it was explained to me. Luke took it pretty well.

Inside, at the kitchen table, I introduced Luke to Arachne and Cerberus, figuring I'd explain who and what they were later. Lastly, I introduced Nicky as his grandmother.

"I was your maternal grandmother's wife," she explained as she pulled out what looked like moussaka from the fridge and put it in the oven. Moussaka was an eggplant and beef with béchamel sauce dish. I had never made it for Luke because Carlo didn't care for it, but I had grown up on it myself.

I held up a finger. "Lukie is a vegetarian."

"Ma, it's Luke or Lucas now." It might have been the thousandth time he'd said it, but this time he had a bit of affection in his tone rather than his usual impatience.

Nicky smiled at my son. "No problem. I'm vegetarian, almost vegan, Luke."

"Almost vegan." Luke chuckled. "Is it cheese?"

"Love the stuff. The fake isn't the same."

Arachne snorted as she returned to her knitting. "They all forget we're predators out here."

"Mushrooms and onions instead of beef?" I asked, hoping to change the subject away from us being monsters. "That's what my yiayia did during Orthodox fasting times."

"I have impossible beef. The fake stuff." Nicky turned to the counter, adding over her shoulder, "Apollonia said they became Orthodox to find the Greek community here. I'm surprised they stuck to it and didn't convert anyone. They've seen the gods."

"What?" Luke asked. "Like Zeus and Athena?"

"Exactly so." The harpy poured some iced tea for all of us.

My son rubbed his brow, blowing his breath out in an exaggerated sigh. "I knew supes were real. I just didn't know we were...latents?"

"Me either until a few days ago," I told him.

"A man manifesting oracle gifts never happens. Usually women become an Oracle," Nicky said. "No one was even watching you."

Luke and I exchanged a look we'd given each other a thousand times since he was little. I wouldn't tell them if he didn't want me to. He gave me an "it's okay ma" smile.

To Nicky, he said, "I was assigned female at birth."

I grinned and ruffled his hair. "He corrected everyone since he was little. Lukie always knew who he was."

"You've always let me be who I am, ma."

He squeezed my hand.

His father was another story.

One we didn't have to think about now.

"You know. There are people who act like queerness is new. It's the other way around," Arachne said.

"They're getting back to the old ways," Nicky agreed.

"Not quick enough, I say." Arachne stopped her knitting. "Do you think your family and new friends are going to be too much for your fiancé? Supes have only been known to mundanes for a little while. You might want to consider saying your mama is sick and you need to care for her."

Luke shook his head. "I'm not going to lie. Juan deserves better than that. He either accepts what we are or moves on."

I couldn't be prouder. That was my boy. Always doing the right thing. Thank goodness he was more like his great grandparents than me or Carlo. Then again, my grandparents had done some lying to me. They had to know my mother's death was fake so she could become Oracle. I wish they'd told me. Lying never spares anyone. I wouldn't have had to live almost forty years thinking she was dead and then and lose her all over again.

"If you'll excuse me, I'll go call him, so he knows I'm alright."

Nicky showed Luke to his room.

I set the table with Nicky when she returned.

"Once a mama, always a mama," Arachne remarked, smiling.

I hoped she had a child and wasn't referring to the myriad of spiders that ran up her muumuu earlier.

Luke rejoined us about thirty minutes later, grinning ear to ear. "Juan is on his way."

I gave him a big hug, excited to have my son and his fiancé in my life, even if it would only be for a short period.

At dinner, Arachne talked to Luke, who was not as afraid of her as I was the first time we met. My kid took so much in stride. I felt a twinge of guilt about that. Carlo and I gave him a life where he had to accept change.

Luke's phone dinged. His mouth dropped when he checked it. "Whoa."

"What?" The three of us asked at once.

"Pops and his crew were arrested this afternoon. The story just broke."

All four of us rushed to the living room.

A dark-haired woman in her mid-thirties wearing a red jacket and pearls sat behind a news desk. "Florida officials report the coast guard, tipped off by ISEA, found the vessel carrying a crime ring responsible for scamming seniors out of millions."

The screen flashed to a picture of Carlo and his buddies in handcuffs, being hauled down the dock by a bunch of cops.

"Good freaking riddance," Luke cursed softly.

Arachne shook her head. "Wish I'd gotten to him first."

I shuddered. "I'd rather Carlo in jail than eaten, thank you."

"You can't be eating people in Milagro Bay," Nicky agreed. "Gives the town and supes a bad name. Hunt your bad guys elsewhere."

Guess that settled that, I thought. Arachne couldn't eat anyone. Here. Dione would be tried by Olympus. Carlo would go to jail. I had my son and my life ahead of me.

"... the ex-wife is still at large. In a recent press conference, Lawless's lawyers claimed that she was the real kingpin, and he is willing to work with authorities on a plea deal to find her. The job may be tough. Ms. Lawless purportedly has many pseudonyms and has run from prosecution before."

"That lying son of a—" Luke began, then he saw my face. Whatever was on it, caused him to pause.

My stomach dropped. I'd lived in a way that made me look like a criminal. How could I prove my innocence?

"Who's Francine Lawless?" Arachne asked.

Before I could answer, a picture of me flashed on the screen. Several actually. My different looks for different towns.

"This just in. Carlo Lawless's lawyer claims his ex is allegedly a supernatural, who has alleged mind control powers, and that she controlled not only the people she scammed but convinced Mr. Lawless and others that they were behind her crimes."

Luke looked at me, his disappointment and shock palpable.

I shook my head. "I can't do that. Your room would have been a lot cleaner."

The joke fell flat.

"Ma—I think you can. Not intentionally, but it was hard to disobey you."

"He's right but not in the way he's saying," Nicky said. "You're a harpy queen. You can make mundanes do as you bid and have a small sway over supes."

I scoffed. "If that were the case, why did my husband cheat and lie and be an asshole to our kid?"

"You never used the power against anyone," Nicky replied.

"You might want to hear this," Arachne said, rewinding the newscast a bit.

The reporter continued, "Authorities are turning the case over to ISEA—"

A knock at the back door interrupted the newscaster.

"I could fly you to the temple. Figure out how to hide you in Olympus from there," Nicky offered.

"I go by my mom's maiden name. ISEA wouldn't know she's Francine Lawless," Luke offered. "Maybe it's someone else."

Someone knocked again.

"Doesn't hurt to run and find out later if they connected the dots," Arachne suggested.

I decided to follow my son's example and take the high road. I was innocent and I was too damned old to run like I had for the past few days. I shook my head and spoke in a firm tone. "No. I'll answer the door and face whoever is there."

We all went together, which made for a packed hallway. Cerberus rose from his newly claimed mat in the kitchen and followed.

I swung open the door. A young woman in her early twenties stood at the back. "I heard the new Oracle arrived last night. I need a prediction."

I almost denied the girl, but Nicky beat me to it. "Predictions are between eight and six. What time is it?"

The girl looked at her phone and grinned. "It's five forty-five."

I shook my head. "Not enough time for a prediction. Come back tomorrow."

I hoped I'd be here to give it tomorrow.

I decided then and there, I'd contact ISEA, not the other way around.

CHAPTER

THIRTY-THREE

Agent Tan had shoulder length hair, straight and silky black. Her bangs were cut blunt across her forehead. She had the type of flawless skin that made it hard to guess her age, but her gray pantsuit gave the impression of someone in her mid-thirties. Everything about her was immaculate and precise. She probably enjoyed writing her reports. She barely parked her butt on the comfy living room chair.

Her partner Agent Roanhorse was the silent, intimidating type. He was the "bad cop" of the duo, or at least liked to give off that vibe. He was probably five or six years older than Tan. His skin had the old scaring of teen acne. However, his strong features had a rough sort of handsomeness to them. Roanhorse wore his long, dark hair plaited, not a single strand out of place. He probably corrected Tan's typos and it likely got under her skin.

"If you're not guilty, why did you run?" Tan asked in a thick Boston accent, setting down a black device. She'd told me earlier that it would record my image.

"I didn't run. Dione summoned me to be Oracle to the

182

Olympians." I gestured to my mother's home. "My mother died, and I came out west to replace her."

"Oracles don't have mind control powers, is that correct?" Tan asked.

"Not to my knowledge," I answered. Oracles didn't but harpies did. Tan hadn't asked about my harpy heritage, so I didn't spill it.

"Who is your father?"

I shrugged. "I don't know. It was just me and my Mom. She got pregnant when she was a teenager."

"As did you," Agent Roanhorse said, accusation in his tone.

"Yes," I answered, unsure what he was accusing me of.

Then he laid it out. "Did you get pregnant on purpose to trap Carlo Lawless into marriage?"

I laughed. "Are you serious? We were kids."

"Is there anything about me that says comedian to you," Roanhorse asked in a cold tone.

I sat back in the sofa and folded my arms. "No. I didn't get knocked up to keep my man. Carlo asked me to marry him. We were just kids, but back then he did what we thought was the right thing."

"Was your marriage unhappy?" Agent Tan asked.

"He cheated on me. Got into trouble, made us move around. It wasn't a life I'd choose if I had mind control."

"Did you use your oracle gifts for all your clients?" Roanhorse asked.

I hesitated. "No. Sometimes I told people what they wanted to hear. I listened and gave the best advice I could. That is what we've done since the days of Apollo's temple on Delphi. There used to be more than one Oracle at a time, but before supes came out we had to reduce our numbers to one." I'd learned that bit from the book Nicky gave me. I'd spent all night reading up on my family business.

"You're a priestess?" Agent Tan asked.

"I am now."

The two agents exchanged glances.

Roanhorse leaned forward. "So, you ran a two-bit sham of a psychic business while Carlo went out and did the real crimes?"

I nodded. "Uh-if that's how you want to put my personal consultant business, yes. If I had mind control, wouldn't I have stolen money from people this whole time? Why would I risk a big scam when I could've skimmed just enough to live well under the radar of the cops all along?"

"It doesn't make sense and your story about your husband's affairs check out," Tan agreed. "How did Carlo know you were a supernatural?"

I shrugged. "He might not. How do you disprove mind control?"

Roanhorse sneered. "There are tests."

Tan cleared her throat. "However, *we* don't think they're necessary. Your story corroborates with your son's and our investigation of Carlo. We think your former husband might have the small magic of influence or may even come from a line of Romans who descended from Suada."

"Who?"

"The ancient Greeks called her Peitho," Roanhorse provided.

Peitho was a minor, rarely mentioned deity, but my grandparents warned me about her. Peitho literally meant persuasion because she was a personification of her name. My grandparents didn't cast a pleasant light on the goddess. She was involved in the Troy shenanigans and liked to hang out with Aphrodite and Eros. The ancient Greeks believed persuasion and desire went hand in hand. These days that would fall under coercion. If the agent's suspicion was true, then a lot about my relationship with Carlo made sense.

"This is all theory," Tan added. "We know his crew are of Mediterranean and Slavic heritage, but Lawless is a very English name and investigators can't find much on him."

"It's as if he doesn't exist," her partner agreed. "He blames that on you."

I looked at the black device recording everything, no doubt. "You want to know what I know?"

Roanhorse leaned forward. "It would be in your best interest, since he's accusing you of being the one influencing everyone."

"The fifth amendment is a lovely thing though."

The agents exchanged glances. Tan pressed the black device. "Because of the nature of Carlo's crimes, this case is high profile. If Carlo is proven to be a supernatural, then it would be the first time one of your kind was tried by a mundane court. It's in Olympus and all supernatural's best interest to prove he's just a mundane. All we need is the family names as many generations back as you know, and we can do the rest."

"What if what I give you proves he *is* a descendant of Peitho?"

"You and your son are in the clear," Roanhorse answered. "Descendants of Peitho are immune to what he claims you did."

I would personally be okay either way. Then again, groups existed who wanted to terminate supernaturals. Would I be adding fuel to their fire?

Funny thing about being an oracle, you could predict everyone's future except your own. If I had control of my gift, I could search Carlo's thread for the best choice to get him locked away and put me in the clear.

Even without omens, portents, or visions of the future, I'd never ratted on anyone in my life. I'd be breaking the only code I've lived by since I met Carlo. However, that was the code of thieves and charlatans. If I were to leave that life, I would have to work with the authorities.

My gut knotted. Carlo had been so much to me. My only family besides Luke. I closed my eyes and took a deep breath, reminding myself that Carlo had not only abandoned me, he'd broken the code first to save his skin. He had no loyalty to me or our son. Carlo only had loyalty to Carlo.

His betrayal hurt, but he never put me first the way Hermes did. The god was expected back in Olympus but stayed to see me through the rest of the trip. I had more than a crew only loyal to me for the money I could bring them.

Carlo wasn't the only person I could trust and rely on anymore. I had family and friends. I had Luke, Nicky, Arachne, Hermes, and even Cerberus.

"We'll start with his real name. Pietro Macri. His parents were Calabrese immigrants—it's unclear whether he was born here or back there. The family stories differ." Tears slid down my cheeks as I betrayed my old friend, lover, and husband of over thirty years, spilling everything he and his late parents had ever told me.

By the time I finished, I had a tissue in my hand.

I don't remember the agents leaving or when Nicky and Luke came in. I do remember them taking me upstairs and covering me with the blanket that smelled like home, before I cried myself to sleep.

THIRTY-FOUR

Luke, Juan, Arachne, Cerberus, Nicky, and I gathered around the television in the living room to watch the last day of the trial. It had gone on for several weeks with both mundane and supernatural witnesses.

The quickie divorce he'd bought wasn't real. Under law, I didn't have to testify against him and that was fine by me. Then again, our marriage wasn't ever real. Francine Walker, the woman Carlo Walker married, no longer existed. I left her behind in that small North Carolina beach town. I went by my real name for the first time since I was sixteen, Lydia Kourakos.

I made spanakopita with Arachne. The spinach and cheese stuffed phyllo dough was the perfect finger food for watching. The boys made us salted caramel and chocolate drizzled popcorn for dessert. Nicky brought out mastika, a delicious, pine sap liqueur she'd brought from a recent trip Greece, to sip as a digestif.

Through Agent Tan I'd learned that Carlo, or his birth name Pietro Macri, had been born a mundane human, but tests showed he had the small magic of influence. There was much speculation on the internet and media about how mundane humans could become supes, none of the theories good for us supes. However, those with the power of influence aren't suggestible, so the question of Francine Walker being the mastermind behind it all was dropped.

Besides, Pietro Macri and his cronies had a mile-long rap sheet of crimes and misdemeanors before he purportedly married me.

Cerberus, laying on the floor, lifted his head. The doorbell for the back rang. Clients usually came to the front, so I got up to get it, rushing to not miss the verdict. Hopefully the jury's deliberation would go on for a bit.

Hermes waited at the back door. "Dione was tried and is being kept in a prison made by Hecate. Zeus, Poseidon, and Hades sent a combined team of their special forces to apprehend Typhon and Echidna. It's over."

"What about the nymph who abducted me from Olympus?"

A dark look passed over his face. "We'll find no answers there."

"Why?"

"Thetis is gone. No shade of her has arrived in the Underworld. A Titan, like the gods, has the power to eradicate someone from memory. My bet is Dione covered her tracks."

My hand flew to my mouth. The nymph's entire existence gone. Thetis wouldn't even be remembered in the form of a shade. I wanted her brought to justice, not killed with finality.

"Ma! The jury is back from deliberation!"

"Shoot. I got to—"

Hermes cut me off by wrapping his hands around my waist, lifting me, and running with me in his arms. I didn't yelp in reaction until we were already in the living room, and he was setting me down. I fought off a wave of dizziness and then focused on the television.

"We, the jury, find Pietro Macri, a.k.a.—" They went down the long list of aliases I'd given the ISEA agents, delaying the already tense moment. "Guilty."

The rest was a blur.

Carlo was going to jail. The Titans were going back to Tartarus. I would get a new chance at life. Something sprang in my chest in the place, sprouting in the place where the ache had been; an unfamiliar feeling that at once brought tears and a sensation I hadn't felt since Luke graduated high school. I remember the feeling and its name, joy.

"You okay, ma?"

I nodded, wiping my eyes with the back of my hands. Nicky poured the mastika, handing a shot to everyone, even got another glass for Hermes.

"To victory!" she shouted.

We all lifted our glasses.

"To my mom starting her new life in the Pacific Northwest," Luke added.

"To family and friends," I said, gaze taking in everyone to finally meet Hermes' dark eyes.

"To love," he said as if I were the only person in the room, or maybe the universe.

I would have to figure out this oracle thing and teach it to Luke. I would have to learn how to be a harpy queen and figure out what other gifts I had. There would likely be more problems coming my way.

However, I wouldn't face them alone.

T.J. DESCHAMPS
Midlife Olympians #2
WESTSIDE HARPY
A PARANORMAL WOMEN'S FICTION NOVEL

Westside Harpy (Midlife Olympians #2)

A Paranormal Women's Fiction Novel

CHAPTER ONE

There's nothing like waking up to a good cup of coffee and a nightmare. A spider the size of a corgi skittered in my direction across the linoleum of the kitchen floor. A few weeks ago, I would've screamed bloody murder at the sight of the creature. If you were an arachnophobe and wished to conquer your fear, I highly suggest living with Arachne and her children as a form of immersion therapy.

Maybe not.

If you're not a good person, you might end up as their dinner.

Cerberus lifted his three heads, one woofed, another sneeze-drooled (don't ask, it's even grosser than you'd imagine), and the third panted, not seeming to understand why the other two heads were in a tizzy.

"It's okay, Spot," I said, but my tone lacked the confidence I tried to portray.

At first, I felt ridiculous calling the three-headed monster hound "Spot," but like Arachne and her children I grew accustomed to it quickly. Upon Persephone's instruction, I had to call Cerberus the name. I wasn't clear why, but she was adamant. Never argue with the Queen of the Underworld, not unless you want to end up her subject. Also, Cerberus acted like a dumb dog ninety percent of the time.

Cerberus's heads whined, panted, and drooled respectively. Then the pooch rose, circled around in his dog bed, and settled down again.

The spider had a sticky note attached to it. In neat blue script contrasting the yellow paper, the note read, "Be down in five."

I could read the note from my chair. However, the spider waited, tapping one of its legs impatiently. Gregory was the most insistent of the children.

"Okay, Greg. I read it. You can go back now."

The spider spun in a circle. It was definitely Gregory. Most of the children would go back to Arachne, satisfied I'd read it. Greg didn't like the little notes. He'd keep spinning near my feet until I took the note off his back.

I shuddered, reached toward him, but then I drew back my hand.

The action excited Greg. His spinning became more frantic.

The thing was I could tolerate his presence, *mostly*, but *touching* the spider was a whole other story. However, if I didn't take the note, there was a good possibility that he would take it upon himself to crawl up my leg. The thought alone made my vision swim and darken around the edges.

I inhaled deeply, closing my eyes. "One, two..."

"Thanks, Greg," my son Luke said.

Clicking sounds indicated the spider scurried off.

I opened one eye, hoping that to be the case.

Lukie had the note in hand, a smirk on his handsome face. When my son gave me that sarcastic grin, he looked like my ex-husband Carlo—or rather Pietro now that he was in jail and using his birth name.

I'd broken the cardinal rule of criminals "never snitch," and told the ISEA agents everything I knew about my ex to save my own skin.

It's a stupid rule.

Besides, Carlo had done worse than snitch. He'd made up things about me. He'd pinned all his crimes his crew had ever done on me, claiming I was a supe and had mind-controlled them since I was sixteen years old.

Pfft.

If I could do that, then maybe he could explain to me his multiple extramarital affairs, him and his crew stealing my savings, and his leaving me for a younger model once he made the biggest score of his life.

Faking that I was psychic may have made me a bit of a scam artist myself, but I'd never done a crime. Not really. Telling people what they wanted to hear and giving them advice under the guise of being able to read the future wasn't illegal, *yet*. The government was talking about passing laws about that, now that supernaturals or "supes" came out of the closet as real. There were a lot of charlatans out there nowadays, gaming people and the system.

I had my own code of ethics. I'd always given made-up readings with my heart in the right place. These people were more like Carlo and his crew, scamming people out of their money.

A few weeks ago, I discovered that I'd descended from the oracles of Delphi and could read the tapestry woven for humanity by the Fates. I just had no recollection of any of my real predictions.

Luke was an oracle, too. He also inherited some of my other abilities. Seems the Greek pantheon got busy with many, many of the erstwhile *mythological* creatures. We were also part harpy and titan, the gods who preceded the Olympians.

My son set the sticky note, still covered with a few spider fibers, on the table and then turned, opening the coffee mug cupboard. "I think Arachne sends Greg so you'll get over your phobia."

"I think she sends Greg because she finds my phobia amusing."

Luke chuckled as he poured some of the steaming coffee into his mug. "You've got to admit it's kind of funny an arachnophobe lives with Arachne and her children."

"Says the guy who asked for a tarantula every birthday."

Juan, Luke's fiancé entered the kitchen. Ready for his commute to work, Juan wore a blue velvet smoking jacket, cream button up, and trousers. His lovely curls were on display, expertly coifed. He flashed us a thousand-watt smile. Juan was definitely a looker. Then again, so was my Luke.

"Buenos dias, familia."

"Ah, my favorite is awake. Kalimera."

"I love when you speak Greek, mami. It sounds so beautiful."

He kissed me on each cheek like a proper son-in-law should.

My heart grew two sizes since they'd moved in.

I loved Juan fiercely, he was so good for my boy. I couldn't wait until the two tied the knot. Unlike some parents, I kept it to myself.

"Don't let Luke tease you. He told me he wanted to get under your skin, mami. He doesn't like spiders either. He just hides it better," Juan whispered conspiratorially.

I pointed at my grown son. "Ha!"

"Not true. Love 'em." Luke placed his hand over his heart, mock offended, but mischief sparkled in his eyes. "Ask Greg."

I shuddered.

My son and future son-in-law chuckled, kissing each other.

Their affection was something I only had in the early days with Carlo. Our marriage had chilled with each affair. So much so, my ex would call me roomie.

I hoped the boys would stay true to each other. Even a modicum of loyalty was better than what I had with my ex.

Juan poured a to-go cup.

Luke got Juan's bento lunchbox ready to carry out the door.

I loved watching their little routine.

"I put some of that leftover lamb souvlaki you liked in there," I said.

Luke groaned. "Ma! He was fine with the tabouli I made."

"I really am, babe."

Juan kissed my son again and winked his thanks in my direction before exiting to the back porch.

Unlike my Luke, Juan was not a vegetarian. I'd slip him meat whenever I could. Luke called it undermining their healthy lifestyle, I called it giving the skinny man a little extra before he wasted away.

"It's such a long commute to Seattle from Milagro Bay. Too bad he can't work from home like you, Lukie."

He threw up his hands. "For Pete's sake, ma. It's Luke."

I grinned. "Okay, Luke."

I liked to tease him with his nickname, but I'd never disrespect him and call him by his dead name. Never accepting our son, Carlo refused to call him Luke.

They hadn't spoken in ten years, ever since Luke had moved into his college dorm. My son kept in touch with me, but I hadn't seen him face-to-face in all that time.

I should've left Carlo a long time ago and followed Luke out west. I could've started over years ago. Now, I was eking out a new life in a new town as a middle-aged woman.

There were a thousand reasons why I should've left Carlo. I just couldn't bring myself to leave the man who stuck with me. Some good my loyalty did. In the end, he left me.

Luke looked at his watch and gulped down the rest of his coffee. "Got to go. Grandma is picking me up for harpy lessons."

Nicky, the local queen of the harpies, was my stepmother. Since my birth mother Apollonia faked her death and married Nicky after she'd abandoned her previous life, the harpy didn't have a hand in raising me, nor was she a part of Luke's childhood. However, Nicky had always wanted to be part of our lives. She stepped in wonderfully as my mother-figure and Luke's grandma.

I followed Luke to the back door.

Nicky flew in just as we walked out. Literally. As a full-blooded harpy, she was born with golden wings and soft golden down, covering her lithe humanoid form.

We greeted her with hugs.

My chest ached when she tousled Luke's hair. "Ready, Lukie?"

He grinned ear to ear. "Yeah. I'm hoping to sprout some wings."

Nicky laughed. "Very few harpies not born with wings can do that."

"My boy is a prodigy," I said, partly because I thought so and partly because I wanted to be included in the conversation.

"Your lessons will come soon," she said, wrapping her arms around Luke.

I nodded, hating that I felt a twinge of jealousy. I didn't know which I was jealous of more: my stepmom getting Luke all day, or Luke getting a day with the mom I'd always wanted. At forty-four, it was pretty pathetic to be jealous of either.

Westside Harpy releases March 15 2023

ALSO BY T.J. DESCHAMPS

MIDLIFE OLYMPIANS

Westside Harpy: A Paranormal Women's Fiction Novel (Midlife Olympians #2)

Westside Titan: A Paranormal Women's Fiction Novel (Midlife Olympians #3)

MIDLIFE SUPERNATURALS

Eastside Hedge Witch: A Paranormal Women's Fiction Novel (Midlife Supernaturals #1)

Eastside Witch Hunt: A Paranormal Women's Fiction Novel (Midlife Supernaturals #2)

Eastside Mórrígan: A Paranormal Women's Fiction Novel (Midlife Supernaturals #3)

ACKNOWLEDGMENTS

I'd like to thank the people of Greece, Travel with Mandy Loo, the tour guides, and Acropolis museum docents.

I'd also like to thank my editors Emily Paper and Rhiannon Rhys-Jones. Thanks for cleaning my book baby up and making her sparkle.

ABOUT THE AUTHOR

T.J. Deschamps grew up in the Endless Mountains of Pennsylvania and has since lived all over the continental U.S. before making Washington her home. There, she lives with three kids, three cats, and an unbothered tortoise named Lily.

Currently, T.J. likes to read, lift weights, dance, and pretend she can garden.

Follow T.J. on social media!

amazon.com/stores/author/B08KGHKV3B
facebook.com/TJDeschampsauthor
instagram.com/t.j.deschamps.author
bookbub.com/profile/t-j-deschamps